DIARY of a FED UP Teacher

Haversaw High School

Diary of a
FED UP
Teacher

Chip Putnam

PROSPECTIVE PRESS
Winston-Salem

Prospective Press

1959 Peace Haven Rd, #246, Winston-Salem, NC 27106 U.S.A.
www.prospectivepress.com

Published in the United States of America by PROSPECTIVE PRESS LLC

TRADEMARK

DIARY OF A FED UP TEACHER

ISBN 978-1-943419-31-9

Printed in the United States of America
First Prospective Press printing, February, 2016
Revised

1 3 5 7 9 10 8 6 4 2

The text of this book was typeset in Adobe Minion Pro
Accent text was typeset in Felt Tip Roman

Previously published in 2014 under the same title

PUBLISHER'S NOTE

After teaching, or surviving, in the blackboard jungle—that has become more of a whiteboard-dotted-with-computer-monitors jungle during my career—I feel that I can offer a real look into what happens inside of a typical American classroom. This diary is fiction in the sense that the characters, the school and setting, and most of the events are made up. However, the events happening nationally and at the state level are all too real, as are the general conditions within classrooms—limited, of course to my personal experiences. These are the fictionalized chronicles of my 2012-2013 school year.

DEDICATION

This work is dedicated to all of my fellow teachers who constantly strive to make a difference in the lives of their students.

1

"Welcome to Haversaw High,
Hornet Valley, NC"

I am William Gregory, veteran teacher and survivor of nine-teen-years worth of service to the state of North Carolina. During this time, I've laughed, cried, yelled, encouraged, begged, pleaded, and taught; but mostly I've laughed. Teaching was a great profession. Any heartbreak was tempered with joy. Over the years, I've written numerous humorous stories concerning teaching and the antics of my students set in the village of Hornet Valley, a suburb of Camelton, in Haversaw County, North Carolina. However, in light of the current hostile political situation prevalent in North Carolina, I felt a need to take a more serious look at my education world.

Within these pages, you will not find any revelations of deep secrets concerning lust and intrigue carried out in the dark recesses of teachers' lounges. Neither will you find teachers trying to subvert the innocent minds of our wards into mindless communist-pacifist-socialist-terrorists. Frankly, when you are dealing with around 180 crazed teenagers, lust is the last thing on your mind and, well, you just don't have the energy for any intrigue. As to teaching any hidden agendas, you don't have the time, what with all of the overt political agendas that pepper the standard courses of study for classes around the nation. All of your time and energy is consumed by the art of teaching and trying to properly present the material the state deems to be vitally important to the future of our students. Outside of a few rare instances, lust, intrigue, and conspiracies to overthrow the government by perverting young minds to a socialist agenda only happen on TV. Instead, teachers, like me, are just regular people trying to make a difference in the lives of the kids they teach.

While lacking in the shootings, sex, drugs, and skullduggery the media has presented as everyday occurrences in our schools, it is my hope that this journal will set the record straight and portray the real drama and struggles that I and my fellow teachers face each day. While maybe not all teachers' story, this is mine.

As one reads this diary, it will be obvious that the first month is not chronicled by date. The reason for this is simple to anyone who is in the field. I was just too blame tired to do any writing during this time. The first month of school can best be described as hell. Consider the following analogy: You're in a blissful, carefree state somewhere in the world, where time and stress are unknown—I like to think of this area as a tropical beach with an endless supply of your beverage of choice—suddenly, some demon from the netherworld sucks you back into the hard world of reality. That's what the first day back at work is like.

For those people who do not enjoy two months off from work, please do not begrudge the poor teachers this pleasure. This is a time of renewal, a time of rest, a time of lowering your stress levels to a point where you don't rip someone's head off of their shoulders. I once confided in a friend that I could not see how the regular worker managed without an extended break. His response was, "William, I've never had a co-worker walk into my office and body slam another co-worker on my desk."

I had to correct him on a few key points. First, it was a student who did that deed, I was talking with a fellow teacher; second, it was a lab table, not a desk; and third, it was the nicest fight I've ever had to handle.

While the event was surprising, I must admit the student in question was extremely courteous about the whole situation. Jennifer, my fellow teacher, and I were calmly talking about changing diapers when Big Bob walked into the room and asked if he could talk to one of my students. As the name implies, Big Bob was large, standing well over six feet.

"Of course, Bob. School hasn't started yet," I said.

Jennifer and I continued our discussion concerning the pros and cons of heated versus cold wet-wipes when I saw John's arms and legs fly through the air. John was, maybe, 5'5" and had a mouth that was at least 5'4" and ran constantly. Big Bob was not the first person to entertain thoughts of body-slamming the little braggart.

"You don't talk about my Mama like that!" yelled Big Bob as he repeatedly slammed John onto the lab table.

With arms and legs flailing in every imaginable direction, John yelled back, "I'm going to kick your ass!"

Once I was able to process what had just occurred and reached the two combatants, Bob quickly released his hold upon the offending classmate, order was restored, and both boys enjoyed a vacation from school.

After dealing with issues such as this one, I hope it is easy to understand why teachers desperately need the summers to recoup their equilibrium. While these situations ensure that I am never outdone at parties when the conversation turns to strange happenings at work, it is stressful in the extreme. So, if any politicians are reading this, please don't try to chip away at summer break. Not only is an extended summer break good for the tourism industry, but it also keeps the teachers from going insane and staring off into space, only to giggle maniacally at odd moments.

The first workday of this school year saw the arrival of a new principal at my school, Haversaw High. There's nothing particularly special about Haversaw High, but it represents any school because basically schools are all the same. Yes, schools come in different sizes and diversity of populations, but once you boil teaching down to its basics, all schools have the same core mission: the teaching of students. While the flavors of the problems are different, all schools face student apathy, unrealistic expectations of parents, lack of funding, etc., all of which make education difficult.

As I was saying, our old principal, Mr. Peace retired at the end of last year while he still had a few strands of hair left. If you think teaching is intense, try being a principal. You get the parents, the teachers, and the superintendent all trying to tell you how to do your job, usually at the top of their lungs. I only get the parents telling me about how I'm screwing up the life of their child. But, the administrators have known me long enough to know I'm competent at what I do. They tend to leave me alone, so I rarely have trouble. Hopefully, our new principal will follow suit.

The new guy, Mr. Flair, is different from Mr. Peace. Mr. Flair has a quiet confidence about him. During the first month, he seemed like a "hands-off" manager unless he needed to be involved. I can respect that trait.

The only real thing of interest I've discovered about Mr. Flair was uncovered two weeks into the school year. Jane, another teacher, came into my class one day at the end of the day. She was on the verge of tears. My concern quickly changed to curiosity when I realized the tears were from laughing.

"You'll never guess what just happened," she said breathlessly.

I said, "Do tell."

She proceeded to spin a tale that had me laughing so hard I almost fell out of my seat. It turns out, she has a very inquisitive fourth period class. While this sounds good, their curiosity has nothing to do with schoolwork and everything to do with the personal lives of teachers. You get classes like that sometimes. Anyway, this class was gung-ho about tracking down the rumor concerning their principal and asked her just as Mrs. Purple (one of our assistant principals who really likes purple) walked into the room. Jane deflected the question toward Mrs. Purple. The students were frantically shaking their heads "no" but Jane carried through with the challenge.

"I don't know the details of Mr. Flair's prior work experience, but why don't we ask Mrs. Purple," Jane said. "Mrs. Purple, do you have any clue as to whether Mr. Flair was ever a professional wrestler?"

To her credit, Mrs. Purple held her composure and answered, "While he's certainly in good shape, I am not privy to his past

work experience either. You'll just have to ask him. Would anyone like a note to the office?"

At this point, the students respectfully declined the offer.
Quick thinking will often get you out of some sticky situations,
and Mrs. Purple is one of the quickest thinkers I know. It is an
honor to work for her. So I'll leave the mental images of principals addressing the school over the P.A. system while standing in
an awkward pose and wearing nothing but a mask and wrestling
tights and move on to other occurrences.

The first thought I had as I surveyed each of my classes at the
beginning of the school year was the impression of looking out
over sea of humanity. At last count, I had 34 students in each of
my regular Earth Science classes. This, by the way, is the lowest
level of science classes we offer, which means these kids need a
lot of help, a task that is next to impossible with 102 kids in three
classes. As I said, when you survey 34 students in a class, you are
indeed reminded of the undulating sea as it moves on its timeless
journey. Of course, when all 34 students are talking at once, the
class bears a strong resemblance to the fury of the strongest of
the ocean's tempests.

The question begs to be asked how this all came about when a
mere ten years ago, a class of twenty-eight was considered quite
large. It all boils down to one word: "Budget." North Carolina has
been hit hard by the recession and tax revenues have dropped.
Compounding the problem was one political party's zealous endeavors to cut taxes at all costs. The one-cent sales tax deduction
enacted two years ago amounted to a net increase of my income
that allowed me to take my family of four out for a big night on the
town at the end of each month. Of course, that is with the stipulation that we went to McDonalds and ordered off the value menu.

This same loss of revenue, however, meant a huge budget deficit for the state of North Carolina at a time when tax revenues
were already down. One estimate put the additional loss at a bil-
lion dollars. I can't rightly say what the final numbers were, but it
equated to a huge loss of money for my school system.

To make up for the shortfall, positions were cut. Officially, we lost very few personnel in this process. However, the numbers of teachers laid off doesn't tell the complete story. Two years ago, four Haversaw High science teachers resigned for various reasons. The Central Office only allowed Mr. Peace to replace three of them. Technically, nobody lost a job; but the reality was we had one less science teacher the next year. With one less science teacher, that's six sections of classes that had to be absorbed among the remaining teachers. Last year was bad enough; but at the beginning of this year, our enrollment had increased and we still had not replaced that lost teacher. So, at the beginning of every class, I look across the sea of humanity hoping and praying I make it through the day without mishap. Being a science teacher who is required to incorporate laboratory experiments into his curriculum, this is a daunting task.

9-12-2012
Wednesday

Over the years, I have noticed that the school year starts out with a honeymoon grace period. This is the time where you're trying to figure out your students, and they, in turn, are trying to determine if they like or hate you. There is usually little middle ground, for the average student is still in that area of cognizant ability where everything is either black or white, or right or wrong.

If the students like you, I can't say that they will do anything for you, but they will at least be manageable. If they don't like you, well, let's just say it is not going to be a pleasant year. I've had both experiences over the years. This process of determination usually takes about two weeks. Now, if you can already sense a deep dislike in the first few days, the school year can best be described as a place of fire and pitchforks.

Two weeks is also the time it takes before students start to open up to their teachers. It is a mistake to view high school students as "little kids." They are not. They have grown into physical adults by the time they are sixteen and they are dealing with many adult issues. I have noticed that the only people who want to continue to treat them as babies are the parents who refuse to admit that time has passed since they last changed their child's diaper. As my own children have grown older, I am beginning to understand this stubborn clinging to the past.

One such student, Cindy, wandered up to my desk today while the class was working on an assignment. Usually, when a student does this, something other than science is on her mind.

"Mr. Gregory," Cindy asked tentatively. "What are we doing tomorrow?"

I thought for a second and responded, "We're continuing our discussion on the planets. If you're going to be out, I'll print you a copy of the notes."

She nodded gratefully, and I thought she was going to return to her desk. After two steps in that direction, she turned and said with disgust tinting her voice, "I'm going to court tomorrow."

Not the reason I was expecting. While I hardly knew her by this early stage of the semester, she seemed like a good kid.

"I'm trying to remove my dad from any semblance of custody over me," she said without prompting.

I made some form of grunting comment, which is the universal acknowledgment that states, "I understand you need to talk, and I also understand that you really don't want advice." Cindy continued to talk for a while explaining how she had lived with her father, but had been more of a "mother" to him than he had been a "father" to her. While Cindy's mother was no saint, she at least could take care of herself. I felt sorry for Cindy. As I said earlier, these aren't little children. They are young adults trying to deal with adult issues.

10-2-2012
Tuesday

We just received word that one of our fellow science teachers has received a promotion to become a science coach at the Central Office. For those of you not familiar with educational jargon, the position of science coach was created years ago when the standardized testing took an ugly turn with "No Child Left Behind." The scores of every possible sub-group of student now came under intense scrutiny. The pressure applied to teachers jumped three-fold because, no matter your views of this piece of legislature, it is very difficult to take a child who, through no fault of his own other than the misfortune of being born with a low IQ, is reading on a fifth-grade level and bring that child to a pre-collegian level where words such as tertiary roll easily off of his tongue. To offer testimony to the Herculean task presented to schools, we were deemed an at-risk school a few years back even though our passing average for the tests was in the range of an accomplished school. It turns out, Mr. Peace, our former principal, made the mistake of having compassion for a kid who was sick on the day one of the standardized tests was administered. Mr. Peace let the boy go home to vomit in a more comfortable surrounding. The only stipulation the principal asked was that he return as soon as he was well to make-up the exam. The boy never returned. As a result, Haversaw High was deemed an at-risk school. Go figure. So, in order to help schools, our Central Office created "coaches" to go into the individual schools and provide support and advice when needed.

Amidst jokes accusing our coworker of joining the "dark side," we're happy for him. (As with any corporation or business, a certain amount of animosity exists between the common workers and the top-management. Schools are no different. Even though we're "all on the same team," the Central Office personnel are often viewed as tyrants seeking to place more work upon the teachers. For their part, the central office personnel probably look upon us as a bunch of whiny jerks.) He's a good man and will do a good job. I wish him luck.

10-8-12
Monday

Today was Crayon Day, the first day of Spirit Week. I'm not certain how dressing-up in your favorite color demonstrates your school spirit, but hey, who am I to argue?

It was slightly disconcerting to have a black crayon sitting in the front row of my class. I kept confusing Bill's cone head he used as the end of his black crayon suit for his hand raised to ask a question. Other than that, the only real casualty was one of the fashion sense. I don't believe it is ever proper etiquette to wear a pink shirt, a different shade of pink pants, and topped off with a third shade of pink hat.

I spent my time in all of my classes teaching how the oceans regulate global temperatures and moderate the climate of both the East and West coasts. Because these were regular level classes, I have learned to define not only the science vocabulary words in my lecture notes, but words such as "moderate" as well. It was extremely sad to see fourteen- and fifteen-year-olds struggling with terms my eight-year-old daughter had on her vocabulary tests. When I pointed this out, in a joking manner, to one class, Maria responded, "That's because she's at that smart school." My daughter Kaitlyn, was enrolled in a magnet school for highly academically gifted kids.

This spoke volumes concerning the problems of our students. Notice, I said "students" not "schools." Maybe I'm biased, but the schools seem to be doing the best job they can with teaching students. However, when a student justifies having a poorer vocabulary than a girl six-years her junior, there's not much I can do. Her problems have now been transferred; they're someone else's fault. "I didn't go to the smart school, so therefore it's okay that an eight-year old has a better vocabulary than I do" figures prominently into this mentality. Instead of a little bit of self-reflection into the root cause of her problems, she blamed anything or anybody but herself.

Along those lines, I also told the students they needed to try to use their vocabulary terms at home. The response by a majority of my students was, "If I use words such as moderate and leeward coast, my mom would look at me like I was crazy!" This highlighted another problem. If we can't get the parents to buy into the fact that it is all right for their kid to be intelligent, then, once again, there isn't much I can do. I see the kids for ninety minutes each day. They are with their parents for the rest of the night. I don't care what any politician or education expert says, I'm out gunned on this one. Unfortunately, I'm just a teacher, not a miracle worker.

Fourth Period was a challenge, but I've lowered my expectations in that class. If I don't have to call the Law down to my room, then it's an acceptable day. A sad testimony, but when you have thirty-four kids in the lowest-level science class and of those kids, twenty-four are boys, and of the ten girls, four of them could out-do most boys, and I'm not even going to talk about the kids with criminal records, then you take what you can get.

2

"Anatomy of an Educational Disaster"

10-9-2012
Tuesday

People cry out that public education is dead. I disagree. It's not dead, but I will agree that it is broken. The breaking occurred as elected officials tried to fix something that wasn't broken. It began with a disturbing report that a large number of NC students were dropping out of high school. Coupled with the scary prospect of only achieving minimum-wage positions for these students, public outcry was loud and furious. So, the General Assembly of North Carolina passed a resolution that dropout prevention would be a major goal for every high school. With this resolution, came the incorporation of graduation rates into the school's annual report card.

In today's world of no compromise, anything less than a perfect "A" is unacceptable to the general public. And what's unacceptable to the general public is unacceptable to the school board, which in turn ensures that it is unacceptable for the principals of the individual schools. So, the orders were given that teachers would do everything within their power to ensure a student's graduation. (That statement is actually a part of our evaluation tool. Note, that the burden is placed, not upon the student, nor upon the parent, but upon the teacher who sees the kid either an hour a day for an entire year, or ninety-minutes a day for a single semester.) While this is a just and noble cause, you must understand that when your attendance book looks like it has developed a bad case of chicken pox from all the absences (I have several students this semester who have already missed over 10 days in a block class and we've only been in class for 12 school days.), it's a trifling bit difficult to ensure the graduation of those students.

Now, the kicker came a few years later as North Carolina, and the United States in general, began to lag further and further behind the rest of the industrialized world on standardized tests. A new cry arose. How could the country that put men on the moon not outcompete the Asians and Europeans on a flimsy test? The public demanded action and resolutions were passed from Washington to Capital City, NC that academic rigor would be our rallying cry. The public cried out, "We demand the best for our students, lest they are incapable of competing in the international arena."

Let's sit back and examine this from a familiar point of reference. Consider a coach who has been given the task of winning the NBA championship, the NCAA tournament, the state championship, or even simply the conference title. Yes, that coach is going to work his/her players to their fullest. "No pain, no gain!" will be the rallying cry for the team. His/her leadership shall inspire the team to excel to new heights. Plus, the coach is going to bloody well get rid of all the dead weight, good-for-nothing members on his/her team.

I can't do that. If you're in my class, you're in my class. "We're stuck with each other," I often tell my classes when they complain about how much work I give them. So, I'm left with the mandate of producing college-level students regardless of their background or if they are even at school. Considering that I have students who cannot identify North Carolina on a map (I had a student last year identify our state as England. That explains my cravings for a spot of tea and my irresistible urge to sing "God Save the Queen.") this can be a difficult task at best. Coupled with the fact that I have students who have already missed ten days of school, the task becomes monumental, and this doesn't address the twelve students in my classes who speak limited or no English. To place it into the realms of sports, this is equivalent of our coach winning (insert tournament of your choice here) with players who cannot hit a basket no matter how many tries they are given and who don't even bother to show up for practice. The idea is ridiculous, but it is what I must accomplish.

So, I try to incorporate academic rigor into my curriculum. For me this is no problem. I'm a nerd who is also a sadistic bastard when it comes to tests. Years ago, one poor girl told me she was struggling with Organic Chemistry in college and calmly recited to herself, "I've survived Mr. Gregory's tests. This isn't so hard." Outside of AP courses, I probably give some of the hardest tests at Haversaw High.

To further muddle up the waters, remember our first mandate that we will ensure every student will graduate from high school. In reality, the two goals—increased rigor and "No Child Left Behind"—are mutually exclusive. The politicians can wrap words around their fingers indicating that both can be accomplished, but I would like to see them try it for themselves. As rigor increases, the academically challenged students fall behind. When they fall behind, a many of the slower students simply quit trying. As a result, they fall even further behind in a vicious self-inflicted cycle which I am utterly clueless how to stop.

All of the educational reforms that have haunted my existence stem from the politicians trying to fix the fact that they set education on a course that cannot be done. The teachers are doing all that they can to promote high educational rigor while maintaining a high graduation rate. But, let's face it, when you have students who think we lost the Revolutionary War and are still a part of Mother England...well, that probably says it all.

10-10-2012
Thursday

I have seen horrors the likes of which mortal man was not meant to see. Today was Opposite Day of Spirit Week. This is the day students dress as the opposite of what they are. For example, if I had an ounce of school spirit, I would dress-up as a jock. When one of my students asked why I did not participate in Spirit Week my response was that I'm not in high school, I just work in one. Some of the participants, such as one of my goth/punk/thug girls removed all of her studs and piercings and came to school in a dress. She looked really nice. That's what the keepers of the secret fire of school spirit imagined when they decided on this day.

The reality was something far more horrifying. Apparently, a large number of our student body is comprised of closet cross-dressers. Seeing the girls dress as football players, or thugs with baggy pants was no problem. To be truthful, a lot of the girls that were sagging, covered up more of their body than they normally show when dressed in their own clothes. Outside of almost yelling at one "boy" for coming out of the girls' restroom only to be answered by a soprano voice exclaiming amidst giggles, "It's me, Jane, Mr. Gregory," the girls were no issue.

The problem arose with the boys. Try to envision the football linebackers in strapless sundresses with fishnet stockings and you can understand why this day was bad, horrifying, dreadful, and downright disturbing. One, very muscular young lad decided to wear an extremely flimsy dress. One of our female teachers pulled him aside and pointed out that either he was chilly or that he was in serious need of a camisole. That's how the day progressed.

Oh, well. I guess it was all in good fun. The next two days should be uneventful. Friday is Wear School Colors Day. The PTSA is also preparing a tailgate party for us during lunch. The tailgating is going to occur in the library so no cars are allowed. That's fine, it's the thought that counts and our PTSA puts on quite a good spread. Tomorrow is Decade Day where you wear clothes from your favorite decade. I even told my students I would participate.

"What are you going to dress-up as?" Sandy asked in disbelief.

"A science teacher from the '90s," I replied. "You'll be amazed at how much he looks like a science teacher in 2012!"

The night before, Caroline, my wife, experienced an emotional nuclear meltdown over school. This is a fairly common occurrence with teachers. I have talked with friends whose spouses are not in the profession, and they express their frustrations over the fact that their significant "other" cannot understand the root causes of the psychological stress. Non-teachers focus upon the fact that teaching is such a plum job. "What's the problem? You get two-months off, holidays off, and you're done by four-o'clock in the afternoon," is often cited by non-teachers.

Let me use Caroline's situation as an example. She has planned a new course for six straight years. Each new lesson takes approximately one-to-two hours to prepare. All the while, well-meaning parents want to know what is scheduled for three months in the future because they are taking their child to Disney World when it's not too hot. When you are planning something new, most teachers don't know what they are doing the next day, much less weeks or months down the road. There simply is not enough time in the day to prepare. The stress begins to build over time until you finally have to let it out.

This year, the state adopted the Common Core of Education (or whatever is the latest incarnation of a list of objectives you are expected to teach in a year). With a new set of objectives comes a new standardized test because we all know the one solution to all of education's problems is to heap more testing on the kids. With new testing comes the expectation that the teacher controls everything that happens with the test scores. Never mind the fact that the teacher is not allowed to look at the test and only has a vaguely worded document to guide them on their quest to impart the knowledge of the ages into the minds of this generation. Never mind the fact that the teacher can figuratively teach their butts off, which he doesn't have because he worked it off the previous day planning, presenting the world's greatest lesson ever delivered to students who are truly blessed to have experienced it, only to see those same students half asleep with doodles drawn in their notebooks and statements of "I'm Bored!" carved into their desks. If they perform poorly on the test, it's the teacher's fault. This problem has been magnified in recent years by the rise in class size.

Now, add to the stress the fact that teachers actually are allowed to marry and have children. So, to use the favored refrains of my students when I assign a project, "We do have a life outside of school." The pressure can reach the breaking point, and sometimes you just need to scream and cry. This has to be done at home because at school, you're expected to present a strong front.

As I said, non-teachers don't understand this. Being a teacher, I fully comprehended the problem and, truth be known, wanted to scream and cry as well. However, I am a male and I did what men on every continent do in situations like this. I tried to rationalize the root causes of the problem. Big mistake. Sometimes it is okay to just shut-up and listen.

As dawn greeted the day with its bright rays of hope and renewal, I was in no mood to enjoy it. In helping Caroline, I had also fallen into a fit of despair. Needless to say, by the time I reached school this morning, I was in a funk.

In my daily ritual, I always check my email first to see if I had a "See Me Now!" e-mail from an administrator. I never know what breach of etiquette I may have perpetrated the previous school day. Years ago, I found myself in the principal's office over a drawing of the first barometer created. It consisted of an inverted tube filled with mercury. One of my students had embellished the drawing and his mother was not pleased with his artwork. Instead of confessing to his crime, he passed the buck saying, "This was what Mr. Gregory had on the board." While I did have the inverted tube displayed on the board, I did not have hair and dangling appendages added to it, nor was my drawing crowned with a spewing fountain! So, I never know when I may have screwed up. Today, however, I wish that it had been one of the dreaded e-mails that I read. Instead, it was an update on the cancer one of our teachers had been battling for years. When you see the word metastasized in describing a colleague, it is never a good thing.

Maybe lackluster students and frustrating curricula are not such bad things after all.

10-16-2012

Tuesday

Today was "Fight Like a Girl Day" in honor of our teacher battling cancer. Because the cancer initially started as a form of breast cancer, the theme was pink. Even though I wanted to show my support, it still felt odd and extremely wrong to raid my daughters' closets in search of clothing. Being that I weigh 230 lbs. compared to their 70 lbs. and 80 lbs., the choices were extremely limited. After much debate, consideration, and a lot of screams of frustration over not finding anything to wear in two closets full of clothes, I finally narrowed my choices down to a pink scarf and a pink *Mulan* nightgown. For the well being of everyone involved, I chose the scarf. I received a lot of complements for my apparel, although I doubt the sincerity of most them. Mrs. Purple was exceptionally helpful with explaining currently accepted fashion trends for scarf wear.

10-18-2012

Thursday

I walked into the office this morning only to be blindsided by our secretary, crying. I've known Kayla for years and it takes a lot

17

to rattle her. She looked up, with eyes bloodshot from tears and simply stated, "They found Steve Jones dead this morning."

Steve was the son of Sally, a fellow science teacher, whom I've known for almost thirteen years. Sally had been bringing her boy around school since he was seven, a practice that while not exactly condoned by the administration wasn't punished either. (Considering the cost of day care, I didn't blame her one bit. We're fortunate to have parents who can watch the girls on workdays.) While not close to the family, I watched Steve grow up. Later, he was a student at Haversaw and would frequent his mother's classroom.

The news hit like a kick to the solar plexus. Obviously, the science staff at Haversaw was devastated. I've been an emotional wreck since I heard it, and each time a teacher arrived, the tears would flow anew as the sad information was told again.

When someone young dies, it feels like the death of an ideal. It's a turning of the social order of things onto its proverbial head. For me, I saw a part of all of my students dying. Images flashed through my mind of people I've taught over the years, and, as I recalled Steve, I saw a part of each of them dying as well. It was as if with one untimely death, a little bit of the illusion of the invulnerability of youth died as well.

Past memories of students who have died surfaced as well. To date, I've had three students die in car crashes, one student die in combat, and one suicide. Today's news ripped open the wounds from a year ago when I received the phone call informing me that Sammy had killed himself. No amount of training can prepare you for facing the empty chair in the back of your classroom.

As today progressed, I was grateful that my students were perceptive enough to realize I was in pain. They gave me the one thing I asked: they behaved. It was one less thing on my mind. A few students offered words of encouragement. I'll cherish both gestures of good faith I received today.

My heart, soul, and prayers go out to Sally. I cannot begin to imagine her pain. I just want this day to end so I can go home and hug my girls. I may even let them go by tomorrow.

I made it through another day. Forget about boldly meeting the challenge of molding young minds to sculpt them into mature, logical, adults. Now, I just want to make it to the end of the day without having my picture plastered all over the front page of the local paper. (For those of you who do not read the paper, it is rarely for good works, dedicated service, etc., when a teacher makes the front page.) I know it sounds terrible to be satisfied with something this trivial, but it's a survival mechanism. Try to imagine that you are in charge of thirty-four employees with no support from management. Simply having your employees show up for work is a success. In the case of a school, the management consists of several branches. One is the Central Office staff that does not want a high number of disciplinary actions mucking up the system's report card. Too many D-1s (disciplinary forms) means too many kids suspended either in ISS (In School Suspension which is the first tier offense for problems) or OSS (Out of School Suspension which is the traditional suspension).

One of Haversaw's sister schools was investigated last year by the ACLU for civil rights violations because it was felt that they unfairly targeted minority students for disciplinary action. The records showed that every case was justified, but the damage had been done. The Central Office issued new guidelines for principals outlining the "fair" methods of dealing with student discipline. Needless to say, the motto "Less is More" has not cut it. The kids aren't stupid, no matter how they act. They know when they can get away with anything short of murder. This leaves me to ponder the question of when will the sense of entitlement end? At some point, people have to accept responsibility for their actions.

The second branch of the "management" consists of the parents. At the risk of sounding like Bill Cosby's father, from his stand-up routine Bill Cosby: Himself, who "had to walk five miles to school in the snow uphill, both ways," things were different when I was a wee lad. I distinctly remember my brother, soaked in soapsuds up to his armpits, cleaning the trashcan with a toothbrush. All the while, our mom was screaming that if it wasn't clean enough, he would have to use the toothbrush that night for his teeth (we're still not certain if she was bluffing) all because a teacher had contacted her the previous day for his excessive talking in class. That's parenting!

While it would be unfair to say that I have not seen drastic improvement in many of my students when I contact the parents, this is becoming more of the exception. It seems that a lot of the parents want to justify their child's behavior, or even blame it on me, the teacher, in some way. For the record, I have never jumped out of bed in the morning with a maniacal grin on my face as I contemplated new and devious ways to make darling, little Suzie's life miserable. The truth-be-told, all I want is to be able to teach my kids a thing or two about how the earth operates.

So, with a class like my fourth period, it is a struggle. As I said earlier, I've had to lower my standards. Now, as long as I can cover a given amount of material and I do not have to call the office to break up a riot, then it's a success.

A fellow teacher told me last week to have a good day.

I looked her in the eye and responded, "With this class, I don't have good days. I have bad days, worse days, and don't even bother to ask days."

10-24-2012

Wednesday

T-minus 1 hour and counting.

"How long are we here?" Fred, one of my students, asked.

"Eternity, plus ten minutes," I replied.

Today we are administering the PLAN test. I'm not certain what PLAN represents, but I'm sure it's supposed to be the latest installment to ensure the best quality of instruction occurs in our schools. How a single test will do this, is a question that is beyond the mere intellect of a lowly teacher. Apparently, by having our sophomores spend three-plus hours filling in bubbles will solve all of societies woes and inspire the teachers to reach for academic greatness. This is a wee bit difficult to accomplish when we have no earthly clue as to what is on this document, which is the epitome of test making. Go figure.

You must pardon my cynicism. I heard this with the ABC of Education, when I began my career, and then again with No Child Left Behind. Both of which were noble endeavors to raise academic standards, increase rigor, and all of those other cool sounding things that basically say we need to be tougher on the kids. My problem with the whole situation arises from the fact that it is by standardized testing in which we ensure that the noble endeavors are accomplished. Once again, this sounds good, but as they say, "The Devil's in the details."

The ABCs ushered in the rise of the EOCs (End-of-Course Exams). By themselves, the EOCs were not too big of a deal. I took the first ones that were field-tested. There was no stress or tension with the process. The teacher handed us the exam and we answered the questions. However, sometime in the last twenty-years, the cause of poor performance shifted from the student to the teacher. If the student didn't score well, it was the teacher's fault. Maybe it was, maybe it wasn't, but after twenty-years in the field, I can tell you that no matter how good a teacher is, if the student comes into the class reading at a third-grade level when he or she is in high school, then that student will not perform well on the test.

One year, I posted the best biology scores in the system and the worst. So, I was pleased to accept the adulations of one of my administrators while I was also chastised for my poor performance from a different administrator. (Okay, you caught me, I made that up.) I did have the best scores in one class and the worst scores in another. The administration, however, understood that it is often the make-up of the class that dictates the test scores, not the teacher. Society doesn't like this. They want someone to blame for their children's low performance other than to hold up a mirror to find the blame. I see the kids for ninety minutes a day. The children's parents are raising them. I must ask, who has the greater influence?

So, back to the details. NC is currently operating under three different programs to improve educational standards. The ABCs are still in effect although the EOCs became the model for measuring growth for No Child Left Behind. Our current model is the Common Core Curriculum, which is the reason we are taking the PLAN test. And finally, the university system places demands on the schools as well which accounts for students placing far too heavy of a burden upon themselves by taking up to seven Advanced Placement classes in a single school year.

To compound the problem, five years ago, various special interest groups demanded that students be allowed unlimited time to take an EOC exam. It was felt that the stress of a timed test placed an undue burden on the child. The result is that students are given four hours to take the things. Until this point, exams lasted either four or two days depending on the school schedule with two exams given a day. If you do the math, you will realize that at four hours each, it is impossible to give two exams a day. Our exam schedule has reached a peak of ten days of exams.

Last week we were in second period for eternity plus ten minutes in order to administer the PSAT to the majority of the kids in the school. Colleges are demanding higher and higher SAT scores, so we've decided to help them by shutting school down in order to give the students a chance to practice with the PSAT. Once again, a noble endeavor. That day, I sat with one class from 9:00 a.m. until nearly 1:00 that afternoon. This severely cut into the time I had for my other two classes. We didn't meet with first period.

Today, Common Core mandates the administration of the PLAN which I think is a version of the ACT, but I'm not certain.

So we're in first period for eternity plus ten minutes. I have first period planning, so I was called in to monitor the kids displaced as their teachers are giving the test. For various reasons these kids do not have to take the exam.

All of which, takes time away from the classroom where the real learning occurs. A few years back, with all of the various standardized tests to ensure the noble endeavors passed by the General Assembly were enforced, some kids missed almost a month of class time taking one test or another. (You have no idea how much I wish that figure was an exaggeration.) So today instead of teaching my kids the mechanics of volcanic eruptions (which is part of the Common Core Objectives for Earth and Environmental Science), I'm sitting in the cafeteria listening to a group of girls give a damn good rendition of "Bohemian Rhapsody" by Queen.

10-25-2012
Thursday

This entry actually started almost a week ago. Last Friday a student of mine came up to me at the end of second period and said, "I can stay until 5:00 today."

First off, I do not mind helping students after school, even on a Friday; but, I do like a little bit of advance warning. So, if my response sounded slightly sarcastic, then I'm sorry.

"That's great," I replied, as neutrally as possible. "But I have to leave at 4:00."

"But my mom said I can stay until 5:00," Samantha replied, slightly crestfallen.

"That's great," I said again. "But if I'm not at South Elementary where my daughter's bus stop is located by 4:00, then she will sit on the curb, with a sad, forlorn look on her face holding a sign saying 'My daddy abandoned me. Please call DSS!' I told y'all that I can only stay after school until four."

It should be noted here that our superintendent rather force-fully informed us that teachers are contracted to work a seven hour and forty-five minute day. If we took time out of work to attend a doctor's appointment we would need to take an hour of sick leave, even if it could be accomplished during our planning period. I noticed that for some strange reason, that seven hour and forty-five minute day did not apply to holding us after four o'clock for unpaid meetings, clubs, etc. Maybe I'm just not seeing it. I've also learned that our esteemed leader does not hold him-self to those same requirements, and we have discovered he has never taken an hour of sick leave to go to the doctor.

Anyway, our workday officially ends at 4:00. It is at 4:00 that I begin my other, more important job of being a daddy. I get to school an hour before classes begin. That's when I expect to do most of my tutoring. We agreed that I would help Samantha until four.

Four o'clock rolled around and Samantha showed up...nice and prompt.

"Okay," I told her. "Get your notes out and we'll see what I can do."

Her face fell as she replied, "I didn't bring my notebook."

Fortunately, my brain kicked in before my mouth did. I'm a lecturer. Every question I put on the test comes from my lecture notes that I expect the kids to write down in their notebooks. I put it all on the boards, but I believe they should be responsible enough to be able to copy something down. A point, I might add, that a lot of parents disagree with. So, showing up to a Mr. Gregory tutoring session without a notebook is like trying to get a house loan with no paperwork indicating that you have a job.

Five minutes later, Samantha returned triumphantly holding her notebook. She then proceeded to sit with an expectant look on her face, waiting for me to impart my wisdom of the ages upon her eager brow. I groaned when I noticed that she didn't even bother to open her notebook. This, unfortunately, is com-mon. Parents will send their kids to tutoring and blissfully expect that all of their academic woes will vanish if the child simply sits in the presence of the teacher. I'm honored, but that is completely unrealistic. It is like saying I'm going to be an NBA great simply because I had season tickets to all of the Deacon Woods games. Of course, with the team's last several seasons, I don't think that was a good analogy.

"Okay," I said, releasing a sigh. "Why don't you open your notebook and let's make sure you have everything. Remember, all of my test questions come straight from the notes."

"Well," she said hesitantly. "I don't always write everything down. Sometimes I just paraphrase."

I don't mind it if the students paraphrase, but when you have a test grade average of fifty, it's not working. "Why don't you try to write everything down for the rest of this test. You know I always give you time if you can't keep up with me."

I learned early in my career that I needed to write things down on the board to slow down my lectures. The more excited I get about a topic, the faster I talk. Writing it helps me keep a pace that it is humanly possible for my students to maintain. I also keep an eye on key students to make sure they are finished before I erase the board and start again.

Samantha wasn't happy about the prospect, but agreed that her method wasn't working.

"How much do you read over your notes?" I asked.

"Uh…," was her reply.

"Why don't you try this," I said to the unspoken answer of "never." "Take your notebook home and read over the notes three times each night. If you have any questions, write them down, and when I begin class Monday with 'Do you have any questions?' you can ask your questions. That way you don't have to spend your time in here when you would rather be anywhere else in the world. Besides, you probably aren't the only one who has questions."

Once again, she wasn't happy about the prospect, but agreed to try it.

I just graded her test. It was a seventy-seven. Her shrieks of excitement echoed in my ears as she ran down the hallway telling her friends.

10-30-2012
Tuesday

I gave a map test today for the mountains and mountain ranges/chains of the world. I've found that it's helpful to have the kids locate things such as the Himalayans, Andes, etc. on a map and then test them on that knowledge. Call me crazy, but I think students should know a little something about the geography of the planet on which we live. My twenty years of experience has given me the wisdom to know that locating individual mountains and mountain ranges is often a difficult task. So, I spent about twenty-minutes going over their map on my 70-inch monitor mounted on the wall earlier in the week.

We actually had a memo sent to us a few years ago mandating that we refer to our public-viewing devices mounted on the wall of our classrooms as monitors, not TVs. This came as a surprise to me as I had recently bought the smaller cousin to my monitor from h. h. gregg and it plays TV shows just fine. Apparently, buying flat screen TVs that can be hooked up to computers and used for classroom instruction was a public relations fiasco as the economy collapsed around four years ago. Now, we have to refer to the things that look remarkably like TVs as monitors. Go figure.

Anyway, I gave the map test today. A large number of kids missed question #1. I had no idea that Appalachian State University was located in both the Rockies and the Andes Mountains.

3

"All Hallows Eve"

10-31-2012
Wednesday

Halloween at school can be exciting. One year I had a cow show up in class. Unfortunately, it was an unseasonably hot day, and I had planned on a nature hike for that day. The poor girl roasted; she didn't have a change of clothes. This Halloween was relatively calm. I only had one gorilla pop into my room to say hello.

On a pleasant note, I gave my Quarter 1 Review Vocabulary Test today. It covered all of the vocabulary, which I had deemed to be the "Core Vocabulary" mandated by the state of North Carolina, taught during the first quarter. It was one of the best sets of test scores my students have posted all year. Maybe there is hope for my state tests.

11-2-2012
Friday

Happy First Day of National Armageddon Week. After years of watching the political process, I have concluded that the world is going to end on Tuesday. Maybe, the Mayans were right after all. (For the record, I do not think the world will end. Personally, I think the Mayans ran out of room on the rock!)

No, the Armageddon, to which I am referring, deals with the fact that my Republican friends believe that the world will end if President Obama wins re-election, and my Democratic friends feel the same way if Mr. Romney wins. So, I've decided to stand in solidarity with my brothers and sisters of (insert political party of your choice here), and I've declared the days leading up to the election as National Armageddon Week. Festivities include learning the Canadian national anthem when we flee the coming catastrophe and (enjoy/suffer through) socialized medicine. We'll also learn that squirrels are not only fun to watch while they frolic in your yard, they are also a good source of protein as you cook them over the open fire you prepared with just a stick, a Slinky, and a picture of what our great land used to be under the reign of (insert president of your choice here).

I think this exemplifies the schism that is building in the American political culture. When we started vilifying the opposition as something less-than-human, then we no longer had to consider their wants and needs. We also no longer had to worry about compromise. Push our agenda through at all cost, and don't even consider the opinions of almost half of the electorate. In my opinion, this is frightening.

In class, we're not allowed to express political views. Somehow, by talking about our views, we are influencing supple, easily manipulated minds, bending them to our political wills. (I wish I was making this up, but I'm not). However, my beliefs do come out, it's impossible for them not to surface. I try to stress the importance of thinking for oneself and not to base a future political affiliation based upon my opinions, but instead look into the actual facts concerning each situation, and ultimately, making their own decision at the ballot box.

Hopefully, after Election Day, we'll return to our senses and start to communicate with one another again.

On a more serious note, I attended the second saddest IEP of my career. An IEP or Individualized Educational Plan is a form used as a basis for providing a framework of support for students with special needs. Each year, the EC (Exceptional Children) Department, must meet with every child labeled as EC and discuss his/her IEP.

The saddest IEP meeting I attended concerned a kid who was guilty of doing something stupid. The meeting was to determine if the stupid act was a result of the student's disability. Sadly, it was not. If it had been a manifestation of the boy's disability, he would have stayed in school. Because it was not, the boy was expelled. I felt horrible. He was a good kid who merely made an unwise decision that harmed no one. As I said, it was the saddest IEP meeting I've ever attended.

Today's was a close second. It dealt with a set of parents who were confronted with the fact that their child's special needs were too great to be dealt with in a regular school setting. The parent's were devastated. We all want our children to be successful, and to have it hit you like the proverbial "ton of bricks" that your child, in all likelihood, would not be able to cope in regular society was heartbreaking to watch. While painful, it really was for the best interest of the child. I just hated that I couldn't do more for the boy.

11-3-2012
Saturday

Normally, I do not like to work at home. After about the fifth year or so of teaching, I had learned the necessary tricks to managing my time so I could leave school at school. Now, it is only during the busiest times at school that I have to bring work home. I wish my work today was a result of a mere hectic schedule, but alas, it was not. Last week we received notification from the central office head of sciences that we must all view a mandatory lab-safety video series. I'm not opposed to training. In fact, workshops have provided a wealth of material for my writing passion. I remember during one such workshop I created an entire kingdom when we were supposed to have been writing our reflections of a particular topic.

One facilitator walked up to me and said, "I've been watching you for the past ten minutes, and I wanted to thank you for embracing the heart and soul of this workshop."

As she walked off, I felt a little sheepish. I had no idea what the actual theme of the workshop was. Still, it was a damn good kingdom.

So, I'm not opposed to workshops, it's just that I'm an arrogant bastard concerning how I teach. My philosophy can easily be summed up as "I'm damn good at what I do, so shut up and let me teach." You have to have this mentality to stand up in front of a classroom of kids and hold their attention for ninety minutes. While I'm open to new ideas, they have to be really good ones to grab my attention.

This training though takes the cake. Seven-and-a-half hours of safety training videos produced by a scientific supply company we'll call Neato-Spiffy Chemical Supply. Needless to say, peppered throughout the training videos are thinly veiled references to products that can be ordered from Neato-Spiffy Chemical Supply. Nice set-up, if you think about it. Scare the bejeebers out of the poor, defenseless science teacher with story after story of lawsuits and then offer a quick solution. Buy Neato-Spiffy Chemical Supply safety gear, and all your worries, which I might add you didn't know you had until you watched the advertisements disguised as training videos, will disappear.

Yesterday, I learned about the proper ways to dispose of mercury. An element that has been banned from North Carolina labs for over five years. Today I'm concluding a stimulating series of videos concerning goggles and the sequel that speaks to the wonders of wearing safety gloves. My heart fluttered when I saw that I still have over three hours left of this riveting saga.

11-4-2012
Sunday

A couple of days ago a fellow teacher, Dave, initiated a conversation in the hallway at church. "You know, William, you are the epitome of the disgruntled teacher."

It caught me by surprise, because I try to be both cheerful and mirthful in my endeavors to educate the young minds of America. But upon reflection, I am pretty well disgruntled. My pay has been frozen for almost five years, and the only increase I've had was this year's 1.5% increase because it's an election year. This 1.5% increase was quickly counterbalanced when Congress allowed the social security tax cut to expire. My class sizes have increased steadily, and I'm supposed to work miracles with the students. I'm tasked with turning them into mature, literate, rational adults, and the students are fighting me every single step of the way.

If I criticize a student, I face a barrage of parent complaints and a visit to the principal's office. Throughout all of this, I get the joy of turning on the TV and seeing how candidate after candidate, and news story after news story, all stating how the current level of educational deficit is my fault. Of course, the solution is to throw more state tests, more training, and more meetings at the teachers who must somehow, find the time to actually teach. So yes, I'm disgruntled.

On top of all of this, a leading public figure recently stated that teachers were parasites sucking the public coffers dry. How silly of me to think that I was a part of a respected professional community, which signed a contract for services rendered. Another backer of the front-runner in the North Carolina gubernatorial race has stated that if Mr. Govern wins, then state retirement pensions were a thing of the past. So my reward for agreeing to lower pay for the past twenty years and taking care of North Carolina's students is to have my retirement dreams destroyed because I'm some sort of monster that had the nerve to think that a contract is binding upon the government issuing it. Well, I would really worry about this, but I have to watch a video on how tie-dyed lab coats and lab-safety posters will keep my students from acting like typical fourteen-year olds. At least I have two workdays at the start of this week. Hopefully, two days wearing jeans will reset my bad attitude.

11-06-2012
Election Day

I'm glad it's over. Now it's time to see what the carnage will be. It's fun to go to work knowing that the governor of your state has your job benefits, if not your job itself, in the cross hairs.

That may be unfair to Mr. Govern, but when your chief financial backer brags that the pension program in North Carolina will be dead after the election, let's just say it does not endear warm, fuzzy feelings toward a candidate. Let me get one thing straight, as a teacher, I do not mind being held accountable for my students' learning. However, don't tie my hands behind my back and then scream at me when the students fail. For example, my smallest class this year has 32 kids. I know some people say the class size does not affect student learning. My argument is that those same people have never set foot in a classroom. Twenty-eight is about the maximum number of kids that I have found can be effectively taught. Twenty-nine if it is a really good, advanced level course. Any number higher and the problems start to multiply. You probably won't find any research on this, but after twenty years of observation, I can tell you that it's true. The best test scores I have ever posted came from a regular level physical science course where attrition had dropped the class size down to twelve.

Speaking of test scores, it has become increasingly popular to test the living-daylights out of these kids. For my earth/environmental science class, I have a list that is twelve pages long, covered with topics that are deemed vital to a student completing the course. All of them are good topics, but I have a whopping ninety days to cover this material. During those ninety days, we have pep rallies, school-wide tests, programs, field-trips, and any other interruption you can name. I'm good, but I'm not that good.

So, my reward for busting my tushy for twenty-years is to have the chief financial backer of my newly elected governor bragging that he's going to eliminate my measly pension check (from a pension fund that is fully funded and is in no danger of running out of money) because I was stupid enough to think that the state would uphold the agreement we signed twenty-years ago when I decided that I would try to make a difference in a kid's life.

11-8-2012
Thursday

I'm feeling a little better now, and I'm sorry about my grumpy attitude earlier. It's just that when you hear it's all your fault that the state is falling apart and by eliminating pensions, further decreasing funding by sending public money to private schools, adding more charter schools that will add a tremendous amount of debt to implement, it can get you down.

I want to issue my congratulations to our governor. He ran a good campaign and won fair and square. I just hope he doesn't forget the workers who have dedicated their lives to the state in his zeal to fix everything he has claimed to be broken.

I think a statement of congratulations is in order for President Obama as well. To mount a successful campaign with chronic unemployment and an economy that is sluggish was quite a feat. Of course, it helps when your opponent fluffs off over half of the American population.

Allow me to elaborate. First, I don't really care what Mr. Romney meant by his 47% comment, a lot of people, me included, took offense to it. Secondly, during the primaries, Mitt Romney courted the far-right and their limited tolerance for illegal aliens. When you basically say, "Go home, we don't want you," you had better hope that the Latino population either didn't hear you or has a short memory. Tuesday night, the world found out that neither happened. The Latino vote was overwhelmingly in Obama's favor. That, coupled with the young vote and the rest of the minority vote, allowed the president to cruise to an easy electoral victory.

As I surveyed my fourth period class, I was reminded of the lesson that I hope America received Tuesday night. With its mix of ten whites, eight Latinos, five blacks, two mixed-race, and one Asian, this class is a microcosm of America. While whites still cling to a majority, the majority is not by much. This majority is shrinking with each year and, in a few short years, there will be no majority race in America. I think it's great. America has been touted as a melting pot of races for decades; now we are on the verge of truly becoming one.

A lot of whites fear this and are clinging with all of their might to maintaining that majority. I have no problems with losing the majority. I've taught in classes where whites were the majority, I've taught in classes where whites were in the extreme minority, and I have classes like my fourth period that is a hodge-podge of races. What I have found is that we are all people. We may have some different cultures or attitudes, but we all want to be treated with dignity and respect. We all dream of success. Losing the majority, I hope, will force white America to face our fellow Americans as equals. This can only be a good thing. Like Mr. Romney discovered Tuesday, the minority vote has finally realized that it isn't really a minority vote at all and it demands respect.

11-9-2012
Friday

Ah, it's Friday. A day eagerly anticipated by teachers everywhere. A day, I might add, that is eagerly anticipated by anyone who gets the weekend off. So please, do not get all high-and-mighty over the fact that I'm looking forward to a couple of days off from work. Just because I'm a teacher, doesn't mean I'm not a human being as well.

Second quarter has started and my students are coming to the realization that this is not a free ride. In fact, some of the kiddies' grades are so low I need a shovel to find them. However, I always provide a glimmer of hope in the fact that if I see a major improvement in their grade, I'll work with them on their semester grade.

We've reached a state of détente in my classes. They don't like the work, and I don't like the complaining, but we've realized we're stuck with each other. This may sound pessimistic, but it's the reality of teaching. We do the best we can and the rest is left up to the students. So, while I may not have inspired them to climb great heights in search of their dreams, I have instilled in them a small degree of work ethic. Most of the kids at least have supplies on their desk without me having to force them. Anyone who's had to work with a group of unmotivated people will realize that this is an accomplishment.

Most of my classes have also come to the realization that, if I don't have to worry about them going out of control, I can make the class more enjoyable. We still have to work, but at least it's not as painful. I'm pleased. With packed, low-level classes, this could have been a horrendous semester. I may be wrong, but I think we're all starting to like each other, or at least not despise each other. It may not be much, but it's a start.

Addendum entry
11-9-2012

Sometimes a classroom can run like a well-oiled precision racing machine. You zoom from one concept to another with the gentle push on the gearshift. Other times, the class can run in one direction, but it's as if you're the driver of the stagecoach, and the horses are frantically trying to take the lead away from you. You're exhausted, but what a ride.

With this being a three-day week leading into a three-day weekend on account of Veteran's Day, my fourth period was like a team of untrained horses pulling a stagecoach where the harnesses had all been cut. Picture eight horses running in eight different directions and the poor driver desperately hanging onto all eight horses at the same time. That's how I feel right now. What a ninety minutes!

11-13-2012
Tuesday

It's amazing what a three-day weekend will do for you. Recharged and refreshed, I'm ready to tackle the challenges of the next week. Of course, let us never forget the sacrifices our brave men and women in the armed forces have done for us. I would like to give a special thank-you to David and his family. David was a great student of mine who lost his life in Afghanistan. Thank you, David.

11-14-2012
Wednesday

"I had an unspoken compliment today," my wife told me. For high school teachers, these unspoken compliments can come in a variety of ways but typically in the following example.

"Do tell," I asked.

"I was working with my algebra kids when I said that they were lucky," she said. "I proceeded to give them a complicated calculus example. One girl asked if it was calculus. When I said yes she asked me if I also taught geometry."

This may not seem like much, but it is one of the best compliments a student can give a teacher. Geometry is the next math class after algebra. When the kid asked my wife if she taught geometry, what the student meant was is it possible to get her again as a teacher. It meant that there was something about her that the student liked enough to want to be in her class again. It's unspoken, but it's things like this that keep us going.

11-15-2012

Thursday

Today I get to teach the lesson I've been preparing for the past three days. Anyone reading this may be thinking, "Three days? Yeah, right. I've seen teachers sitting in the workrooms reading papers and drinking coffee. Don't complain about planning time. That's paid goofing off time."

I feel that it is necessary to point out a few facts. One, every job of which I am aware has breaks during the day. That is, everybody except elementary teachers have breaks. Their breaks consist of walking their students to specialized teachers and running to the bathroom. By the time they are finished, it's time to herd the students back to the classroom.

Second, a lot of those teachers "goofing off" are P.E. teachers. Let's face it, it isn't too difficult to plan the P.E. curriculum. I can picture it now, a group of P.E. teachers are sitting around in a classroom trying to determine ways to enhance core curriculum retention of the basics of kickball. It takes about three minutes to grab the bag labeled "kickball supplies" from the storage room and head out to the field. What the majority of the world may not know about P.E. teachers is that coaching a sport is part of their job description. They are present at the school for all hours of the day and night. I am not about to begrudge them a twenty-minute coffee break. One coach who teaches across from me uses this time to be an advocate for his players with college recruiters, spending hours of his "goofing off" time trying to obtain scholarships for his boys.

My planning marathon was a result of the core curriculum re-alignment, or whatever we're calling it these days. One of my unpacked standards (don't worry if that term doesn't make any sense to you, I don't understand it either) states that I have to teach the concept of geological time from the perspective of NC's geology. A noble gesture, indeed, and I'm sure the great planners of the Old North State are happily sitting in their offices envisioning the students gaining an ever deeper understanding and appreciation for our state as they track it's formation through the geological time scale from the Cambrian to the Holocene. However, you should try finding the highlights of the Ordovician Period of the Paleozoic Era of the Phanerozoic Eon for NC in any textbook. It's extremely difficult because for a large part of this time, North Carolina was underwater. It was only at the end of the Paleozoic Era that the state emerged in all of its glory during the formation of Pangaea.

As a result, this took a lot of computer legwork. I also love to use pictures to supplement my teaching, so additional time was spent finding images to highlight these key events in NC history. It's been a challenge, but I've enjoyed it. Where else are you going to learn that the events that occurred over a hundred million years ago shaped the NC landscape? I was also able to explain the occurrence of the natural gas trapped in the shale deposits, which are making the news with the controversial fracking technique of drilling, formed when sediments filled in huge basins that formed as Pangaea broke apart during the Triassic Period. Learning new things is fun; you should try it.

On a different note, I spent around ten minutes talking with Cindy about how it's not her fault that her boyfriend became suicidal when she broke up with him last night. A large part of teaching—the part of teaching not covered by any standardized test—involves counseling the kids. Sometimes a troubled child, like Cindy, just needs someone to listen to them and reaffirm that the situation is not her fault. I should also note that I wound up giving the students the last ten minutes of class to decompress from nearly ninety-minutes of lecture on the aforementioned geological time scale in NC. It was during this time that I was able to help Cindy. I may be heartless, but I'm not cruel.

11-19-2012
Monday

Caroline suffered a nasty incident today. A kid spit in her water, and the class watched as she proceeded to sip from the cup for the duration of the class. Later a girl approached Caroline and informed her of the transgression. The administration and the kid's parents were furious and the perpetrator was punished severely.

This leads to a question: What other job do you have to watch your drink like a hawk? If a worker spit into his boss' cup, he would be fired immediately. In education, it is viewed as a joke, albeit a sick one, but a joke none-the-less. Kids will be kids, is a mantra I have heard repeated over and over and, to be perfectly frank with you, I'm sick of it. Just because my wife and I chose to enter the teaching profession does not mean that either one of us forfeited our rights as citizens of the United States. This was sick, gross, and completely unacceptable, and, if it had happened in a restaurant, the worker would have been fired, if not arrested.

However, because the kid is a student, Caroline is expected to continue on as if nothing had happened. While yes, the boy was punished, he should have been charged as well. I guess Caroline could have pursued the situation further, but it should be automatic if a student breaks a law, they are charged with a crime. Maybe I'm wrong, but just because you're a student does not mean that you are immune to the law of the land.

11-20-2012
Tuesday

Imagine the day before the three-day Thanksgiving Break: my classes were running wild with visions of cranberry sauce and turkey flitting through their minds. Science was the farthest thing from their concerns, and it was safe to say that the Hottentots were running amok. Just as my fourth period had settled into a state of equilibrium known as organized chaos, the power went out. Fortunately, I'm old school and still use the board. My friend, Amanda, has everything on her computer: lecture notes, PowerPoint presentations, digital animation, everything. While, yes, she gets good marks on her observations, her class had to shut down. She resembled the proverbial chicken missing a head as she ran from room to room asking what were we going to do with no power. With a wicked grin on my face and much to the delight of my students, I opened the blinds and continued teaching geological time. To date, I have never had to deal with my whiteboard crashing or going out of commission when the lights went out. That's 21st Century Skills for you.

11-26-2012
Monday

Mondays are hard, but Mondays after a break are terrible. The whining, the complaining, the grouchy attitudes, and that's just me and Caroline getting moving in the morning. Needless to say, the students don't like it any more than the teachers do, but we have to press forward. State tests do not allow for any downtime just because neither you nor your students are in the mood to work. As it is, I don't think I will finish the material mandated for the common exam in January.

I've had two pop-in observations today. I don't know if it's a system requirement or a state requirement, but all of the principals have to perform a mandatory number of quick observations to check up on life at the school. In other words, to get a feel of what the teachers are doing or not doing. I don't mind and will usually include the principal observing me into the lesson. I think they get frustrated because they have to enter in their data on their tablet or phone while they are observing and having to answer questions from me. Today, I was able to teach Mrs. Purple the origin of the nickname "Lucy" for *Australopithecus afarensis*. In case you didn't know, she (who may have been a he) was named for the Beetles song "Lucy in the Sky with Diamonds." Mrs. Purple did balk when I asked her to join in on a rousing rendition of that classic.

On a follow-up note, Caroline was greeted at her classroom door by the father of the kid who spit in her cup last week. Head downcast in shame, the boy followed his dad into the classroom. Let's just say the boy's life has been hell for the last five days. He was extremely remorseful, but it still doesn't erase the fact that he offered one of the worst insults possible in this country. After the class period, Caroline sent me an email saying that it was harder to deal with the students in class who knew, but refused to warn her. I can understand. I guess it wouldn't be professional to hock up a loogie in their cups and then make them drink it.

11-27-2012

Tuesday

I'm tired. Motivation levels are dropping fast. If I were Captain Kirk, I would be worried that we were suffering from a dilithium crystal shortage. But, I'm not and what I'm suffering from is a shortage of sleep. Family issues have crept into the scene and situations long thought buried have reared their ugly heads again.

In this case, it's in the form of a well-intentioned cousin trying to bring peace to a family where I haven't spoken more than ten words to my father in almost six years. As a result, I spent half the night tossing and turning and the other half of the night dreaming about witches attacking Chip and Dale. (I'm a little worried about the last one, but I'm prone to weird dreams. One time, I dreamed of zombies rising out of the prairie to terrorize Ma, Pa, and Laura. It would make a good short story.)

The net result of all of this is that I'm tired, cranky, and just plain tuckered out. With education, this doesn't matter. You're expected to be at your top performance no matter how you feel. Normally, this isn't a problem for me. I find solace, as crazy as it sounds, in my students. I will often lose myself in my teaching. I hope this is the case today. But right now, I'm just tired.

One reason why teaching can be fun happened today. I have a kid, we'll call him Pepe, who just moved here from Mexico. He speaks very little English. Two of my boys have taken him under their wing and, for better or for worse, are attempting to teach him English. Pepe has really come out of his shell. Today, Pepe pulled a trick on one of the boys, we'll call him Bob, which resulted in the appearance that Bob wet his pants. Everyone, including Bob, thought it was hilarious, although Bob did declare that he would have his revenge. It should be an interesting week.

11-30-2012
Friday

Sometimes I'm prescient. The week was indeed interesting, but not nearly in the manner in which I had thought. Today, contrary to the popular myth that hard work never hurt anybody, I found out that my laundry tried to kill me. Not in the smell-so-bad-it'll-knock-your-socks-off (which by the way should have been in the aforementioned laundry) kind of way, but in the leaving-you-gasping-for-breath-as-you-clutch-the-dresser-hoping-desperately-you-won't-pass-out-from-the-pain variety. It's been my lot in life to never be able to report that my injuries were from fighting off would-be vampire assassins, heroic feats of athleticism, or even from activities that have you smiling for days afterwards, but I'm not telling a soul how it happened. No, I pulled at least eighteen muscles in my back loading the blasted clothes dryer. As I pushed myself upright, wincing from the spasms of my aggrieved back, the thought of "I don't think I can do this" ran rampart through my brain.

Unfortunately, I had missed school yesterday for a funeral that had added to the interesting week. Thankfully, it was the sudden death of my great aunt, Agnes, and not for someone else. The thankfulness comes from the simple fact that Aunt Agnes was suffering from Alzheimer's and had been reduced to the point of wondering if her daughter, who had recently celebrated her 40th wedding anniversary, knew the nice man who kept coming with her to the nursing home. The sudden death was far better than the slow wasting of the memories that define a person. I have seen this far too many times through the eyes of friends.

The funeral was nice, but it was held in Greenville, SC, a distance that took around three hours to drive one way. Needless to say, it would be really difficult to take a half-day of time off for the visitation and funeral which were both held on Thursday and were completed around 2:00, drive three hours, and make it back to school by 12:00, which was when I needed to be there to claim only a half-day of leave.

With the missed day on Thursday, and the doctor's appointment for Mckenzie on Monday, there was no way I could miss today, even if I could barely walk. When you miss multiple days in the real world, your co-workers may grumble, your boss may complain, but no real harm is done unless you're an accountant at tax time. For a teacher though, it is a different matter entirely. They say, "While the cat's away, the mice will play." This is absolutely true with teaching. Teaching is tough, but substitute teaching is a nightmare. When I retire, I'm planning to throw my cellphone into the nearest river to keep Haversaw High from calling me in to cover classes. For a teacher to miss three days for something other than major illness or the illness of a child is next to unthinkable. This doesn't even address the issue of the state-mandated curriculum and exam. If I'm not at school, even though the students should be able to work independently to gain a deep insight of a particular topic, they don't learn a blasted thing. With teeth gritted to ward off screaming, I waddled to the van and set out.

A pulled back is a horrible injury. Walking, breathing, and sitting—all can bring about extreme discomfort, and all are done during the course of my day. I believe it is safe to say that today was not pleasant. Each step brought fresh torrents of pain through my body, and it was not helped by the fact that three of my students decided to make fools of themselves yesterday. Well, three trips to principal office did a lot to calm the rest of the class and while not joyful, the class did learn how electricity was generated so they could charge their phones to see the latest installment of "Cats Wearing Underwear" posted on YouTube. Exhausted, I managed to pull together sub plans for Monday and dragged myself out of the door. I expect the couch, the heating pad, and I are going to become good friends this weekend.

12-4-2012
Tuesday

I went back to school today. Monday, Mckenzie had a few appointments with doctors, one of which included a flu shot. These appointments pretty much took up the entire day. Actually, it took up around three hours of the day, but because those three hours spanned the magical 12:00 p.m. time of a half-day, I had to take an entire day of sick leave. The ironic thing is that Mckenzie was fine at the doctor's office that morning, but woke up today with a 102-degree fever. So, it's back to the office for a flu test tomorrow.

The weekend was good for my back although it's still sore and stiff. At least I'm not gasping in pain every time I move. While better, my back has not healed. Of course, a co-worker needed a heavy piece of equipment from my room this morning. I told her it was fine for her to have it, but she would have to come get it. I normally would have carried it to her room, but I'm not about to go back into the pain I had just escaped for a portable oven.

My return to school was a little less intense than last week. This time, the sub left no descriptions of the class. I'm going to assume that they were darling little angels. They certainly weren't confessing to anything.

On a sad note, I found out that one of my students was placed in the psych ward at the hospital for attempted suicide. It didn't surprise me. Now, this isn't from some super teacher fifth-sense. My suspicions came from using plain logic. The kid had been placed on homebound services for an extended absence with no reason given. This usually means the psychiatric ward at the hospital. It was upsetting.

I knew the kid was bipolar, but I liked the kid anyway. We always got along well; and if sometimes I carried on a conversation with three different personalities, it was fine with me. However, at times you could sense a darker persona lurking behind the kid's eyes. It appears to have found a way out. The sad thing was that there was absolutely nothing I could do to help the kid. That doesn't sit too well with teachers not to be able to fix a student's problems. It's akin to a doctor watching a patient slowly fade away. It makes me mad. I just hope the treatments succeed where I could not. To be perfectly honest, I miss the kid.

More years ago than I care to count, a friend of mine retired. It is common for retired teachers to return and gloat...*oops*, I mean share in past memories, with the teachers struggling to reach that long-sought-after goal without making it on the front page of the Haversaw Gazette.

I asked this friend what was the best thing about retirement.

"Well," my friend responded in the long drawn out manner known throughout the South as a fanfare before the dispensing of great knowledge gleaned through the ages. "It's great to get sick and not have to pull together lesson plans."

On the surface, this sounds crazy. He could have answered about the joys of sleeping late, the wonders of spending extended time with the grandkids, the shear bliss of not having 100 plus kids a day screaming out your name as they desperately need something. But, to a fellow teacher, not having to make out sub plans makes perfect sense. Thankfully, I work in a system with an automated system for calling substitute teachers. In the past, I've spent hours calling sub after sub only to be told they were already booked. I eventually decided that it wasn't worth it, and I went on to work and infected all of my students.

After you get a sub, you have to provide detailed plans. No matter how hard I try, the sub always seems to mess up what I left. At first, I complained bitterly about this only to be answered by more experienced teachers with an infuriated nodding of the head that conveyed without words, "You'll see." I found out when I first had to cover a class for a fellow teacher that my co-workers are idiots who can't write out a decent set of directions if their life depended upon it. Then I looked at my own plans left for a sub and realized I fit the idiot category as well. What was painfully obvious to me was not so clear to a complete stranger who didn't understand "Get the maps out of the cabinet." I'm a science teacher; I have sixteen cabinets. I knew which one held the maps, but my sub didn't.

So I learned the hard way that what is clear to me is not clear to someone else. As a result, when I am out, I try to be as detailed as possible. This takes time, and when your classes are ninety-minutes long, it takes a lot of time to pull something together that (1) the students can do without you because the minute the teacher is not with them, the students' brains turn to mush, and (2) will take up the entire 90-minutes. They say idle hands are the devil's playground. I can tell you from personal experience that a class with nothing to do makes idle hands look like the Pearly Gates of Heaven itself.

This task was made even more difficult by the development of the twenty-first century classroom. This program was designed to equip all of the classrooms at Haversaw with technology so we could astound the students with a big, 70-inch monitor for the computer. Complimenting the monitor was a surround-sound system complete with a set of microphones. Somehow my voice blaring over a set of speakers is supposed to enhance student learning. The problem with this concept is that I'm loud. Early in my career, I taught in a room with an AC unit that had a few ball bearings loose in the fan system. It bore a strong resemblance to a B-52 bomber preparing for takeoff whenever the system was activated. After countless work orders, I simply learned to talk over it. Let's just say it is not a good idea to amplify my voice. The one time I used it, students in the next county wondered who was suddenly teaching them biology. The technology cart was supposed to contain an electronic slate as well, but mine was donated to another teacher long ago. Hers had broken, and the central office forgot to budget for the replacement costs when the twenty-first century technology broke. I figured my twentieth century board would work just fine.

The pros and cons of investing in technology is a topic for future discussions with someone else. I've said my piece on the issue long ago. One pain-in-the-butt issue with the technology, though, is that they took away all of the VCR and DVD Players. Of course, VCR is dead as road kill, but we still have quite a few good DVDs. As long as I am present, this is not a problem. I just run the DVD on the computer. However, the central office does not trust the subs with access to the twenty-first century technology, so the substitute teacher, whom we will hire to care for 100-plus students, is not given an access code to the computers. Try to figure that one out.

This discussion of substitute teachers was necessitated by the fact that Mckenzie had the flu. When you have to go to work and leave a sick child in the care of someone else, even a grandparent, is the pits. Now, I have to pull something together for Friday in case Mckenzie is still sick and, just for the record, I'm not feeling too good myself. What a week! I wonder if I can get a teacher to stream Netflix into the room.

12-6-2012

Thursday

There's nothing like spending the night with chills induced by a fever. Mckenzie was identified with the flu yesterday, so it doesn't take an epidemiologist to figure out that I probably have it too. I had the flu shot over a month ago, so it has taken the brunt of the virus's force away, but I still felt bad all day. I dragged myself to school today, not from any sense of obligation to Haversaw High, but because I had material that needed to be covered for the test tomorrow. Current indicators are that my students are not cheating, so I don't mind having a sub give my students a test. Those indicators, by the way are their test scores. If they're cheating, they suck at it.

Modern over-the-counter pills can work miracles, so the day wasn't too bad. I believe my fever broke last night anyway, but it was still a lousy day.

To cap it all off, I had a student teacher observe my class today. Why, in this current political mess that has mired education, anyone would want to enter the field is beyond me. I suppose people said the same thing about a young, snot-nosed college student named William Gregory twenty years ago. As fate would have it, the soon-to-be teacher, appeared in the doorway of my fourth period class. Well, I had told her cooperating teacher that if the girl had wanted to see the ugly side of teaching, then this was the class she should see.

I would like to say that she saw a master teacher expertly wielding all of the tools of modern education as he molded young minds into an intellectual force to challenge the world. However, that is only seen in the movies. The reality is much different. You push, you yell, you plead, until you either reach the end of the lesson or your endurance. Most teachers are exhausted by the end of the day.

I dream of being the teacher whose life is turned into an inspirational movie that comes to describe an entire generation of educators. People would watch the film, admiring how the teacher would skillfully control the class. While unruly, the class would instantly fall into a waiting silence at the slightest quip of the master teacher, waiting to be filled with the teacher's wisdom. After I began teaching, I realized what should have been glaringly obvious. Those kids were paid actors and the whole scene was staged. It's easy to control a class when you wave money in front of them. I had wanted to be like John Keating in *Dead Poets Society* or exhibit the genius of Glenn Holland in *Mr. Holland's Opus*, but the reality is that I'm just a schmuck trying to make a difference and possibly teach the kids a thing or two about how the world works. If I inspire a few kids to science greatness, then so much the better.

12-7-2012
Friday

Well, I was out again today. Mckenzie was actually doing much better, but with her tendency to get pneumonia, both Caroline and I decided to play it safe and give her plenty of time to recover. On the flip side, I really needed to be out. I won't go into details but they consisted of: I felt like CENSORED and had to make the mad rush to the toilet.

I wisely decided to change my plans for the day, considering that I stayed home paying homage to the porcelain god. While I did have Netflix ready to stream an informative video on the journey of Lewis and Clark, I had also watched an Indy film earlier in the week. Let's just say the "suggested films" that popped up as a result were not ones I wanted wildly circulated among my students. Fortunate for me that I went back and altered my plans because Mckenzie had streamed *Angelina Ballerina: Love to Dance* after I had left school and that was what popped up in the recently watched section of the screen. That would have gone over well. Of course given my student's interest in earth science, it may have made for an extremely enjoyable day for them.

12-11-2012
Tuesday

When you start your lesson with the title of "What Happens When I Flush?" you know it's either going to be a great lesson, or the lesson of your nightmares. For my second and third periods, it was a great lesson. We talked about the processes of treatment for drinking water, as well as the other end of the spectrum with sewage treatment. While a dirty topic, it's one that we all need to understand.

Fourth period was an episode out of *Beavis and Butthead*.

"HU, HU, HU," Butthead said. "He said poo."

You get the picture. It was long, but at least it is done. Between the immaturity and the kids who can do no wrong, it was not a pleasant afternoon. If you are not familiar with this category of kids, they are the ones that you can watch acting like an idiot, but when you call them on it, they scream that they didn't do anything.

On a more serious note, a friend of mine has received an official reprimand. Apparently, one of her students has accused her of yelling at him. The funny thing is, no one can corroborate the story. If a teacher does something wrong, then they should be punished, but I do think due process should be followed. Nobody should be reprimanded on a single accusation.

12-14-2012
Friday

I can't talk about this now, except to say my prayers are with the people of Newtown, CT.

12-17-2012
Monday

A couple of days have passed since the shootings in Newtown, CT. I have held my own children tightly more times than I can count, simply thankful that they are alive. All of their little faults and quirks that were so aggravating a few days ago have been revealed for the triviality that they are.

Words cannot express our nation's feelings at this moment. Be they parents, teachers, gun supporters, gun haters, or just your regular citizen, all have shed tears over Newtown, CT and the senseless violence delivered into the town's midst. I will leave it to far more talented authors than me to eloquently state what can be summed up in the simple statement that it is horrible.

The teachers at Haversaw have saluted our fallen comrades and all have asked, either aloud or silently, "Could I have done it?"

Could I have confronted the gunman as Principal Dawn Hochsprung did? Would I have had the courage to shield the bodies of my students as Anne Marie Murphy and Victoria Soto did, dying in the hopes that maybe one child would be spared? For me, and I do not think this is cowardly, I hope and pray I will never learn the answer to these questions. But, for the brave souls at Sandy Hook Elementary, the answer was an emphatic YES. They have my admiration and may God welcome these heroes, with their students, into His loving arms.

With any event such as this, your "recliner generals" have vehemently begun calling for action. If this had been done, it would have been averted. If only they had done something different, those kids would be getting ready to enjoy Christmas. I'm afraid that nothing would have prevented this tragedy because, as far as I can tell from what's being released, the shooter did not do anything to broadcast his intent until the bullets were being fired.

One chilling revelation came out of our discussions at Haversaw. The gunman was twenty-years old. He had gone through the post-Columbine lock-down drills for schools. He entered the school, killed anyone trying to stop him, forced his way into a classroom, and proceeded to massacre the kids who were huddled exactly where he knew they would be. That, my friends, terrifies me.

12-18-2012
Tuesday

I would really like to write a longer entry, as well as work on our journal chronicling the big family trip last summer. Because I've used many pictures of the drive through a large chunk of our country in my class, I wonder if I can claim the trip as a business expense.

One kid asked, "Mr. Gregory, do you take vacations with the idea of using the pictures in your class?"

My answer was, "No, and yes."

No, I do not plan a vacation with an idea of using them in my classes. However, when I see a situation, which could prove useful in my teaching, then, yes, I will use it. During the time of one course, my students have watched Mckenzie and Kaitlyn grow up in various photos embedded in PowerPoint where I've used them for a scale reference to highlight some specific point. My two favorites are one taken by Caroline showing me and the girls climbing a cliff in the Badlands, and the other has Kaitlyn riding a cheesy fake pony in a field of high grass prairie in Minnesota. When I flashed this image on the monitor, which looks a lot like a TV, one of my kids yelled out, "Hey, it's a cute kid and some creepy fat guy!" I was waving my arms like a moron in the background. I may be nerd, but I do like to have fun.

I'm also trying to write a short story all the while collecting more rejection letters for my novel length manuscript. So, I would like to have written more on this project, but I'm too blamed tired. Just to make things fun, on top of all of my personal projects, and the tasks of teaching and parenting, I'm not sleeping well. Let's just say, this does little to provide the energy needed to fight my students in my unceasing battle to attempt to get them to care and take responsibility for their lives. Combined with my training meeting for administering the Common Exams (They used to be called MSLs for Measured Student Learning, but everyone made fun of them and called the tests missiles. So, the state changed their names to CEs. For every single test, the teachers have to be trained because we can't be trusted to read a set of directions.), which took until 5:00 pm today, and Mckenzie and Kaitlyn's activities, I'm pooped. It's frustrating for a struggling would-be author not to be able to formulate two complete sentences in a row and I tend to ramble when I'm tired and write never-ending sentences that make Caroline wince......Oh, well. I think you get the picture. I'm going to bed.

(A Fond Farewell)
2-19-2012
Wednesday

We received an email from our principal yesterday reminding us to please be prompt for the meeting today with the superintendent. I've been pleased with Mr. Flair's performance so far this school year. He's soft-spoken, but when he talks, you had better listen. So, with that insight firmly entrenched in my psyche, I recognized a command when I read it. The mental translation read, *Be on time or else!*

Needless to say, I was on time. I can't blame Mr. Flair. Nobody wants to look bad when your boss stops by for a visit. I think it is easy to forget that principals are people, too.

I had assumed Dr. Super was touring each of the schools, giving his farewell address. After twenty years of leading the Haversaw School System ship, Dr. Super was retiring. Outside of the bizarre schedule Haversaw High has been forced to follow for the past three years, I have few complaints with the superintendent. He has had a limited impact upon my world as a teacher. In reality, no superintendent truly affects a teacher's life. That isn't their job. The superintendents hire the principals who directly interact with the teachers. The superintendent's job is to be the face for the school system. It is the superintendent's job to communicate with the school board, the county commissioners, state government etc. to provide funding for buildings and the everyday running of the school system. It is the job of the superintendent to provide the overall plan of the system to enhance student learning. When they are directly involved in the running of the school, things have gone horribly wrong. Thankfully, I have never had to deal with that situation. The best superintendent I have ever had the privilege of working for was Dr. Pre-super. We met him at the start of his two-year stint and he said, "Hello, my name is Dr. Pre-super. I look forward to working with you." We didn't see him again. He did his job and let us do ours.

During Dr. Super's presentation, I waited anxiously, with notes in hand to record his momentous words of parting. He discussed various types of test scores, which if I went into details would bore you to death, that exemplified Haversaw's excellence. It was a pleasant experience. But all the while, I was waiting for the goodbye speech. I had even come up with a great title for the journal entry: "A Fond Farewell." Suddenly, Mr. Super said goodbye and left. The meeting was over. That bastard ruined a perfectly good journal title. I think I'll include it anyway, even though it really wasn't a fond farewell.

4

"Countdown to the Apocalypse, End of Days, or the Zombie Apocalypse"

12-20-2012
Thursday

The last day of school before Christmas Break coupled with the eve of the Mayan Apocalypse, what more could a teacher ask? Of course, because I learned long ago that the best lesson plan for the day before a long break was to give a major test, it probably will be the End of Days for some of my students' grades. Let's just say it's never a good sign when multiple students enter your room on the day of the test asking, "Now, what was the test on?" My second period's grades weren't too bad. With a five-point-in-case-I-screwed-up-the-key-curve, the first question asking what is H_2O, and the final question stating...

Q. Merry Christmas, Happy Hanukkah, Happy Kwanza, Feliz Navidad, Happy Holidays, etc.

A. This is the answer. Only enter the letter A; if you enter anything else than the letter A, I can't help you. You're on your own with this one. It is your destiny to enter in the letter A into the CPS (Classroom Performance System...aka clicker). "Luke," Obi Wan Kenobi's spirit voice called out. "Forget about the Force, the answer is A."

Only ⅓ of the class failed. This should tell you something about my semester so far. Especially given the fact that this is my smart class.

Other than students hyped up on candy and prophesies of destruction, the day was pretty good. I did tell the students that if they were concerned about the upcoming end of time predicted by the Mayans, to bring me all of their money and I would personally see that it was put somewhere safe in the Bahamas. I think we are all in need of a break from school. T-minus 5 hours until the end of the world and failing that, T-minus 6 school days until the common exam.

12-23-2012
Sunday

I learned something new today. I found within an article in our local paper quotes by our newly appointed school board member stating that he was not a gun fanatic. He is a member of the NRA as well as Grassroots NC, a statewide organization dedicated to insuring that no new gun regulations are enacted in NC. However, Mr. X wanted to make it emphatically clear, he was not a fanatic.

It has been my experience that if you have to state that you are not something multiple times, then it probably means that you are. I will refrain from the cheap shot of asking Mr. X—if he is not a gun fanatic—to please explain it to me, as well as the families in Newtown, CT why any sane human being feels that it is necessary for every single person in the USA to have multiple civilian grade M-16s loaded with thirty-round ammo clips filled with ammunition designed to cause maximum damage to whomever is unfortunate to get hit by it. I can more than understand the desire to protect your home, but six shots from a .38-caliber revolver will stop just about anybody. But, let's face it, if more than three people are invading your home, they are probably going to get you regardless of what type of gun you possess.

All of this, unfortunately, is irrelevant to the role of future school board member. I hardly think the NRA is going to use Mr. X as an agent to push the wonders of the Second Amendment into Haversaw High's curriculum. Considering that the arrival of state-mandated testing heralded the establishing of specific curricula across North Carolina, there is very little that Mr. X's political views concerning guns can influence daily operations in the schools of Haversaw County. The one relevant piece of information I gleaned from the article stated that Mr. X was in support of providing uniformed officers and deputies on the campuses of all the schools in our system. Currently they are only stationed at high schools and middle schools. Having the properly trained personnel would show the world that we truly do mean business when it comes to protecting our schools. Yes, it will cost money, but I firmly believe what happened in Newtown could have been prevented if a law enforcement officer had been at the school.

This is a matter far too weighty for a mere teacher to be able to comprehend. Now, I have to plan the surprise Christmas gift of the year. (Okay, you got me. At least in the Gregory family, it's the only surprise gift this year.) Our goal is to get the girls to church without them realizing the suitcases in the back of the car. This, I'm hoping, will be easier than it sounds. One, my girls are incredibly silly on Sunday mornings, which has triggered more than one unholy thought as we're frantically getting out of the house. Two, we have an SUV with three rows of seats. The suitcases are all the way in the luggage area in the back. I threw a bright pink blanket over them just in case Mckenzie and Kaitlyn glance back there. If we can pull this off, the girls are in for a treat when we leave church and head towards Concord, NC. We're not planning to inform them of our destination and present until we pull into the Great Wolf Lodge.

It's after nine o'clock, we're pooped, and everybody except me is asleep. Our plan worked like a charm. Caroline and I had concocted some lame excuse for the need to go to Concord Mills Mall. It wasn't until we had turned in the wrong direction and the Great Wolf Lodge was in sight that Mckenzie and Kaitlyn realized something was amiss. It was great. As is so often the case with Caroline and myself, when we leave Haversaw, all of our cares and worries are left behind. It was nice to let the apprehensions over the shootings (and the ramifications that our media was sifting through gun policy beliefs of a candidate for a routine appointment for a school board vacancy), and worries of my students' performance on the CEs (as well as how that will reflect upon me) fade into the background. With each passing mile, the weight became less and less upon our minds. This is why we always try to plan a trip at the start of breaks. It helps us to relax. On a pleasant note of conclusion, we all had a great time today.

(Author's note. It may seem insensitive to include a surprise Christmas trip in the same entry hinting at gun control laws in relation to the shootings in Newtown, but it's not. My heart and soul cry out for the victims; but, as is so often the case, life does not stop even though your world has ended. Frankly, I don't think this is necessarily a bad thing, because, once you realize the world has moved on, you can begin to rejoin it.)

(Follow-up entry 1-2-2013: Mr. X has withdrawn his name for consideration. Allegations have arisen, including his stance on gun control, that he feels necessitates removing his name for school board.)

(The New Year Begins)
1-3-2013
Thursday

It is customary upon the start of the New Year to reflect upon the past year. For the sake of artistry, I had planned to do this promptly at the stroke of midnight. However, I was engrossed in writing a short story and completely forgot. Then the mundane issues of life—cleaning, laundry, playing with kids, etc.—interfered. So, here I am, three days later, reflecting upon the past year. Maybe this says something about my innermost psyche, or maybe not. Who can tell? All I know is that my New Year's Resolution is to maintain a positive disposition.

My first reflection as I start the school year is one of relief. For the first time in twenty years, I do not have to answer questions concerning the belief that the Mayan's had predicted the end of the world. For a brief time, I am free of doomsday questions. For that, I am truly grateful.

That feeling of exuberance is tempered with one of trepidation. I read in the paper yesterday, that North Carolina's new governor elect plans to push through his initiative tying teacher pay raises with student performance on standardized tests. I have already discussed that I have students that cannot identify the United States, Canada, or even the Haversaw River that flows less than three miles from the school, on a map. I have beaten the proverbial horse to the point that not only is it dead, but I have also flayed the skin off of it, concerning the issue that a lot of kids are coming into school with more emotional baggage than they, or I, know how to deal with. When you have taught a kid who didn't finish her homework because her mother's boyfriend was pimping her mother out to pay for their crack addiction and the girl couldn't take it anymore and left, knowing the steps of the Kreb's Cycle in cellular respiration is the least of her concerns. The summation of my concerns for this topic occurred yesterday. I was trying to give my students a pep talk, to motivate them for the upcoming Common Exam. (By upcoming, I mean that the light they currently think indicates the end of the tunnel and a means to their freedom from my class is actually the CE express barreling down upon them.) An exam that is 25% of their grade and whose scores will figure prominently in my evaluation, I might add. When I informed the kids of this, one of my students looked me in the eye and said, "Well, I guess you're screwed then."

Businesses can fire employees who do not perform up to their expected levels. I can't. My mandate, as a teacher, is to teach all who enter my room. I can't kick them out; I can't simply tell them to never return. I have to try to reach them. In twenty years, I can say that I have truly touched and inspired one student. Unfortunately, that was during student teaching. I've been searching for the magic formula you see in movies concerning teachers ever since. So, if Mr. Govern and his subordinates are successful in their endeavors, then my student's prophesy is true. I guess I am, truly, screwed.

Not wanting to sound like gloomy Eeyore, I will say that it was good to see my students again yesterday. I'm not much of a sentimentalist, but I do miss the little boogers during the breaks. One girl, however, was not too thrilled to see me yesterday morning. She had been lying in bed dreaming peaceful dreams, when her mother's screaming at her to get up had rudely awakened her. Both mother and daughter had thought school resumed on the third of January, not the second. When the school bus for the neighborhood's middle school passed by their house, the mother realized school was, indeed in session. Thirty minutes later, the girl was sitting in my room. I can't blame her for being a little grumpy.

By 8:30 a.m. I had already blown my New Year's Resolution. The simple mistake of opening my email account caused the transgression. Among the various emails for male enhancement ads and promotional advertisement for upcoming events at the local coliseum, all of which were supposed to be blocked by our email's filter, was an email from the central office. Its title was Common-Exam Constructed Response Training and Rubric-Enhancement Session. Even after reading the article, I had no further clues as to the actual meaning of the email than I did before I opened the email account. I did, however, gain an undeniable urge to disable the thesaurus function on the computer of the author of the email. So if you should happen to see me enhancing any rubrics for a constructed response, please let me know so I can document it for a later date.

5

"Not Everyone can be the MVP in the NBA Championship"

1-4-2013

Friday

We live in a sports-dominated society. If you disagree with me, compare the salaries of teachers who mold young minds and prepare the future leaders of America with your NBA stars who throw a ball through a metal ring. Whether this is right or wrong, is irrelevant, although I would like to see what it is like to be in the top 1%. But alas, I was born with a severe deficit in the ability to throw, dribble, or hit a ball. This is not an entry whining about how unfair sports verses academia is in this country. I merely use this as a metaphor that everyone should be able to understand. The best is by definition better than everybody else.

In sports, we get this. In education, we do not. We think that everyone should be the MVP of the top league in the world. Every student should make an "A," every teacher should have the highest possible evaluations, and every school should have the highest possible rating.

This may sound harsh, but it is an impossible dream. Everything is compared to something else. If everything has the highest rating, you change the rating so everything is spread out again. If not, it is a meaningless measurement. I'm happy when my students do their best. I couldn't care less what their scores are. When my classes have too many high grades in a class, I increase the rigor. My job is to challenge my students, not to give them warm, fuzzy feelings. But, this is not an entry concerning the focus of our schools.

No, this is an entry concerning Haversaw School system's newly appointed school board member. This appointment was brought about when a school board member become a representative in the General Assembly for his district and his replacement removed himself from consideration on account of not being a gun fanatic. I wish both of them the best of luck. Unfortunately, the school board seat was not up for re-election and the now state representative did not resign it until after the election. So our county commissioners were given the task of appointing a new school board member. Because the Republican Party holds a majority on the board of commissioners, it was a foregone conclusion that the school board pick would be a Republican. I'm okay with this even though I'm a Democrat. The Republican Party campaigned well and won the majority fair and square. So they picked a Republican appointee who I will refer to as Mrs. School.

From her biography I read in the paper today, she seems like a nice lady, active as a stay-at-home mom and a valued participant in the PTSA. Unfortunately, having a clue as to how a school operates is not a pre-requisite for the job of school board member. If it were, she would not have made the statement listing her biggest priority is to ensure that every teacher receives a distinguished rating on the teacher evaluation.

This is where the MVP analogy comes into play. A few years ago, the state of NC implemented a rigorous evaluation tool designed to only award those who truly deserve it the highest or distinguished rank. These are the teachers who are teaching state or national-level workshops. These are the teachers who are attending state-level conferences, providing insight for the actual policies being developed. The proficient rank was designed to be awarded to your highly competent teacher. To be proficient means that you are an excellent teacher. Below proficient, you receive a "developing" status and are placed on an action plan. Failure to comply with the action plan, which is intended to raise you to the proficiency level, means you're fired.

As I said earlier, if this were a sport, the concept would be understood. The MVP is the best possible player in a field of many good players. However, Mrs. School thinks all teachers at Haversaw should be MVPs. But, if you understand the evaluation tool, you realize this is impossible. Everyone can't be the leader. If we could, whom would we lead? Absolutely nothing would be achieved. Consider a room of cats trying to build a quantum box*; it won't happen. An evaluation tool that rates everyone at the highest level is worthless. It is either too easy to achieve the highest ranking or you simply assign the highest level to everyone, and the hell with the evaluation process.

This sentiment bleeds into the classroom. Parents feel that if a class average is below an A, then something is wrong. But, in reality, the class average should be a C. If too many kids receive an "A", then the teacher is too easy. The grade becomes meaningless. While I applaud Mrs. School's desire to have excellent teachers in her schools, I hope she will take the time to learn what the scores really mean. I just hope Mrs. School will visit the schools, talk to the teachers, and gain an appreciation of what is needed to run a school before she makes any decisions.

   *If you missed this pun, look up Schrödinger's Cat and its relevance to quantum theory.

1-7-2013
Monday

Mr. Flair won some brownie points for style and deftness today. We were reviewing the exam schedule, which is a major mess. It drags out for seven days with a day at the end labeled exam make-up day/regular class day. Keep in mind, this regular day is a week after I have given my last exam, but I'll go into that later.

First off, there is no excuse for kids to have to endure seven days of exams when they can only have a maximum of eight classes. But in the infinite wisdom of somebody who is wisely remaining incognito, we have two days of Common Exams scheduled for Thursday and Friday of this week. These are the exams that count 25% of my kids' grades and will be used to evaluate my performance. However, they really aren't the official exams, according to the exam schedule, even though this grade is what I will enter into the exam slot of the grading program. Confused yet? So, my kids, even though they have finished their exam, will have to come back the next week to sit through my class doing an assignment for a course whose grades will have already been calculated. Logic would have dictated that we give the CEs during the exam slot, but logic doesn't apply in this situation. The state wanted to have constructed responses to promote rigorous academic training. (Constructed response is jargon for essay questions. Essay questions have a negative connotation, while constructed responses sound new and hip.)

They say "the devil is in the detail," and this is an apt description for what has occurred. Those constructed responses have to be "graded" but due to budget shortfalls, tax cuts, etc., the Old North State is a little strapped for cash. So, they do not have the desire or the money to pay people to grade these constructed responses. This means it is the responsibility of the teachers to grade them. Now, this shouldn't be a problem. I give constructed responses (even though I call them essay questions) to my classes all the time. I assign the essay question first, and then, as the kids are finishing the multiple-choice section, I grade the essays. By the time the class is done, I've completed the essay grades. A simple computation and the overall grade is done. Everyone is happy and general rejoicing abounds.

But wait, teachers are low-down, shifty scum who can't be trusted to accurately grade an essay question. In all honesty, with so much pressure placed on us for these tests, I can guarantee that some teachers would cheat. So, we can't grade our own papers by ourselves, or anyone else's papers unless we are in an open room observed by a testing coordinator and possibly an administrator. Rumors abounded that Jimmy Carter was to be flown in to ensure the integrity of the grading process, but I'm not putting much stock into those. To further muddy the waters, two different teachers must grade each constructed response. In a nutshell, this will take time. So, we are giving the CEs early.

At the risk of sounding like an old fart, back when I was in school, they would have told us to stay at home if we were already done with our exam. But, this is the 21st Century, the Century of No Personal Accountability. We can't tell the kids to stay home because that would mean the parents would actually have to be responsible for their children's welfare and conduct. A school system was sued a few years ago because two children got into a fight on a day they were told to stay home. Needless to say, it's a mess.

This brings us to this morning's faculty meeting. John, our resident hothead who will voice the questions a majority of people would like to, but are afraid to ask, pointed out that, in essence, those teachers who have CEs will become babysitters. Our former principal, Mr. Peace, would have gotten frustrated at this point.

Mr. Flair, however, just smiled and said, "Don't say that too loud, John. The babysitters will protest if they have to take a pay cut to match our salaries."

Today, also highlighted why teachers groan at the concept of being judged by student test scores. At the risk of bragging, I'm a damn good teacher. All year I've busted my tushy aligning my instruction to match the common core curriculum and essential standards of the earth/environmental science course. I have taught, shown PowerPoints, assigned guided practice (that's jargon for making the kids do a worksheet), created thought-provoking analogies, and all the wonderful stuff a good teacher is supposed to do to motivate his students to achieve the greatness they deserve. To culminate this great semester in the academic achievement of my students, I prepared an exam review highlighting all of the concepts the state of NC deemed was important to the well being of earth/environmental students everywhere.

At one point, I reached a high level mark when almost 50% of one class was actively working on the review. Keep in mind, their exam is less than five days away. The rest couldn't be bothered with doing the review, no matter how much I pleaded, coaxed, and downright begged.

Of the ones who were working, I received an interesting collection of questions, which highlight why it is not only unfair, but possibly criminal in my opinion, to judge my teaching on the performance of my students on a test I neither made, nor have seen.

"Did we actually cover this stuff in class?" one asked.

"Why, yes," I replied.

"But it's not in the book," the student said.

"I know," I replied. "All of the material is in your notes. Remember, I told you the book does not cover the entire Common Core curriculum. I've had to supplement a good bit of stuff."

"Oh," the student said. "I didn't take notes for this. I did my math homework."

Another student asked, "Mr. Gregory, is the Earth a planet?"

I may be wrong, but I'm pretty certain I covered that one little aspect of the course.

Another student asked, "What's the name of our galaxy?"

The list goes on and on. So, for anybody that wants to compare me to a manager, I say this. Let me staff your store with anybody off of the street, regardless of training, background, or proficiency with the English language. Now your store is staffed and you have a goal of X amount of product to sell; however, you cannot fire any employees. No matter how they perform, whether they show up for work, whether they have a caustic attitude, they are your workers and you, the manager, must personally assure that all of them will be Employee of the Month. Oh, incidentally, you will only receive a bonus if your store exceeds expectations for sales. Silly me, I forgot, your CEO deemed that bonuses for managers were considered to be wasteful spending even though he is toting the wonders of merit based pay to the media.

That last bit was based on the fact that Haversaw High has exceeded growth in every category established by the state of North Carolina for the past thirteen years. Not only have we exceeded growth, we have been in the highest category of growth for the past three years. State law mandates that teachers in schools that exceed growth will receive a bonus. I haven't received a check for at least six years. A victim of the recession was the first excuse, now we're just wasteful government spending. At the risk of sounding whiny, that just doesn't seem fair.

1-8-2013

Tuesday

Two things have occurred today that make me realize why I'm doing this. The first was this morning. Out of the blue as we were getting dressed, Caroline said, "One of the highlights I've had in my classes this year has been the kid who spit in my drink."

This was a little surprising. I'm still mad at the little cretin. Caroline expressed that the boy has shown genuine remorse for his actions and has tried to make up for his mistakes. Not by being syrupy-sweet, but by trying hard in her class. Now, he is one of the kids who "get" math.

Part of our jobs as teachers is to help kids grow into adults. Caroline took the moral high road and forgave the student. (She's a far better person than I am.) The kid realized he had made a major mistake and had worked hard to turn his attitude around.

It reminded me of another kid I taught years ago. He was a total clown in my class. Despite the juvenile behavior, I liked him. One day, I yanked the kid into the hallway after yet another stupid prank. All of his friends thought it was hilarious.

"You realize they are playing you for a fool, don't you?" I yelled once we got into the hallway.

"What do you mean," the kid asked. "Those guys are my friends."

"Just wait," I said in warning. "You're going to really screw up, and then we'll see where those friends are."

True to my word, the boy did something truly stupid and was in serious trouble. Amazingly, those "friends" thought it was all funny, and laughed at the foolishness of the boy. When the boy was finally allowed back into the regular classroom, he had completely changed. I kept up with him for the remainder of his years at Haversaw. He graduates this year and is planning on attending NC State.

The point is we all do stupid things. Usually at the bidding of people who think it's great fun to watch someone else get into trouble. Once we grow up, we realize how shallow those friends were. This is what Caroline has observed and it is powerful to know that you had a hand in it.

The other situation occurred once I arrived at Haversaw and heard the angelic voice of one of our secretaries over the PA system informing both me, and every other teacher at the school that I was late for my meeting. It was a meeting for a girl, I'll call her Donna, who had all but failed my class, and I was late because I couldn't get the stupid grading program to boot so I could print off the progress report for the girl's aunt.

The fact that Donna's aunt was at the meeting, and not her mother should speak volumes. I already knew most of the details, and I will not share them here. Needless-to-say, the girl's life was a wreck. The aunt finished by thanking all of us at Haversaw for caring for her niece. Donna's a smart, likable girl, and I've hated watching her self-destruct. It was one of those meetings where I'm going to make sure I give Mckenzie and Kaitlyn an extra hug tonight for just being themselves. Sometimes, we don't know how good we've got it until we see someone who definitely doesn't have it.

I've ranted and raved over the injustice of being compared to a business. I have made the analogy that in a business I would have fired Donna long ago. She's missed over thirty days of my class, and we only meet for ninety. For those of you who like math, that's over 33% of the class she has not attended. Fair grounds for dismissal, I would think.

However, this is where schools, particularly public schools, are different. We don't fire the dead weight. If that were the case, both Caroline's student and Donna would not be a part of our classes at this time. No, we don't fire them. We show them compassion and, more importantly, we give them second, even third chances. We take them all, no matter what their backgrounds, no matter what type of horrors are occurring in their lives. We take them, we love them, and we try our best to teach them. And just maybe, some of these "losers" as the world would label them, might just survive and go on to become productive members of society. For a lot of them, we're all that they have. That's why I do this day in and day out. I've always been a sucker for the underdog.

1-10-2013
Thursday

This was supposed to be an entry talking about the joys of test administration. How the sheer enjoyment of watching kids' brains ooze out from their ears stimulates my neurons to the point of near bursting. In case you did not know it, teachers are not allowed to do anything during a state exam. We can't grade papers, we can't read, we can't eat, we can't drink, etc. I'm not certain if we are allowed to undergo cellular respiration or not. I've been too afraid to ask. Needless to say, we find things to occupy our minds like counting to a thousand in Chinese. If you don't know Chinese, all the better. Then you have the pleasure of inventing a new language in which to count to the a *flarglosbo*. I've read accounts of prisoners in solitary confinement. Test administration is about like that, only without the food or bathroom privileges.

All thoughts of my inconveniences disappeared quickly when I read the following email from one of our secretaries.

A member of Bob Smith's family called to inform us that Bob passed away last night shortly after midnight. The family will keep us updated with arrangement and service details.

Please keep Bob's family in your prayers.

I didn't teach Bob, but I knew that he had been battling cancer. This, of course, is not something you want to have attributed to anyone under the age of eighty. His cancer was a particularly aggressive form of the disease that was wiped out last year by chemotherapy only to return with a vengeance this year. From the way his friends have rallied around Bob and the tears I've observed from those same friends and his teachers, he must have been a great kid.

For some strange reason, it doesn't seem to matter how well my kids will perform on their CE this afternoon. They will leave school, go home, and, I hope, receive a loving hug from their parents, grandparents, guardians, or whoever else is raising them. Who cares about test scores? In the end, these scores are simply numbers on a piece of paper. It is how you are remembered when you have gone that is a true measure of how successful you are. We won't have test scores for Bob, but from what I've seen, he was successful beyond measure.

(Reflections on the Semester)
1-16-2013
Wednesday

I would like to be able to state that my kids performed beyond my wildest dreams on their Common Exams, but I can't. Not because they stunk up the charts, but because those devils in the details have shown themselves yet again. We just received an email saying our exams will not be graded until January 25th at the earliest.

It sounds great to have a written component on the exams of our students. This will ensure that we accurately measure student learning by eliminating the chance involved in multiple choice, or "multiple guess" as it is colloquially called. There is a high degree of truth in the belief that Lady Luck can be the patron saint for numerous students taking multiple-choice tests. I had one student who admitted that his score of 87 on my state biology test, given many years ago, was the result of a zig-zag pattern that allowed the boy to finish his exam in under ten minutes.

The benefit of multiple choices is ease of grading. Students take their exam, the teacher counts and bags the answer sheets, the test coordinator delivers the tests to a grading site, and teachers get exam results the next day. With open-ended, hand written, or "constructed responses" as we're calling it today, somebody has to sit down and grade the blasted things. I spent nearly four hours grading the little boogers this past week. For the record in case someone with the authority to fire me actually reads this memoir, I did not mind doing this even though I can't rightly say I enjoyed it. I hate grading papers. I know it's weird, but I would rather be thrown into an empty swimming pool containing rabid wolverines than sit down in front of a set of papers needing to be graded.

In that four hours, I managed to grade four sets of papers, which was considered a good pace. It would take more time than I wish to spend to go into all the details to explain, but on Monday, I had a four hour long planning period so I could grade those papers. During the rest of the week, I did not have a planning period. So, I have been unable to grade any more exams. State law dictates that these papers have to be graded in a common area with the test coordinator or duly trained surrogate in attendance. Furthermore, at least one other trained adult must be present as well. This is to ensure that the tests are graded fairly and accurately, i.e. the teachers don't cheat and change answers. The threat for this is real, considering that our new governor wants to pass legislation that will tie future bonuses and pay increases to student performances on these Common Exams. So, I hope it is evident that I can't just pick up a stack of papers and grade them at home. As a result, it will take time to get the thousands of papers graded at Haversaw High. Then the state will have to analyze the results before a grading scale can be released. As I said, the devil is in the details.

Now is the time for reflection. During this semester, I have experienced many highs and lows. I taught three, ninety-minute regular earth and environmental science classes this semester. This is a schedule that is often given to teachers the administration wishes to force out of the school. While tenure protects teachers from frivolous dismissals (For example, a teacher cannot be fired for being too "hot." I, for one, am glad for the protection because I'm fairly certain my good looks would have resulted in my dismissal many times over.), but it does not protect us from other, punitive means to force a teacher to resign. Classroom assignments, schedule, extra-curricular activities can all be used as weapons by a vindictive administrator. A schedule such as the one I endured this semester is a classic example, although I volunteered for it, lest you get any ideas that my job was on the chopping block.

Regular earth and environmental science is the lowest level of science we offer at Haversaw High. The kids are rough, typically hate science, and really would rather be anywhere else in the known multiverse* than sitting in (insert class of choice) class. Over the years I have taught arsons, rapists, drug users, drug dealers, fighters, and any other negative connotation you could name. Overall, these classes are a challenge, especially when you combine them with current cuts in staff that have resulted in my average class size of 32.5 students. For the past 90-days, I have started each class wrestling with the students to get them to settle down, spent the majority of the period persuading them that it is their best interests to actually do something in a class that is required for graduation, and I have ended each class period basically telling the class to shut-up. During this time, I was expected to teach these kids the intricacies of the earth, the dynamics of weather, and the subtle dance between life and the environment, all the while knowing that how well these kids performed on their Common Exam would determine my value as a teacher. Then, after I dragged my tired-and-battered body (okay, that was a little bit of exaggeration) home, I got to look forward to repeating it the next day. That's the issue with teaching low-level kids. It's not the individual; it's the mob. The mob can take kids who are great at home and turn them into apathetic, hyperactive, disrespectful, little monsters. (I don't understand how an individual can be apathetic and hyperactive at the same time, but I've seen it time and time again.) That's the challenge of teaching low-level kids. It's the fact that you have to fight them in a constant battle that only ends on the last day the class meets. Over time, it wears a teacher down. Needless to say, my stress level has been higher than I care to admit, I have high blood pressure, my sleep has been haunted by nightmares about my classes, and I have been grumpy for most of the semester.

However, for all of the trials and tribulations, I would gladly do it again. I have watched children grow with maturity, I have helped my older students enter into the adult world fraught with responsibilities, I have seen students succeed by hard work, and I hope I have laid the foundation for a successful academic career for my freshmen students. I can truthfully say that I am proud to have been a part of these students' lives. That's not to say that I'm not looking forward to teaching all Honors Chemistry next semester, but I have had many quality moments in my stint teaching all regular earth science.

On a follow-up report, I have to note that Mrs. School, our newest school board member, has dropped all references concerning teacher evaluations. Hopefully, that means that she will be willing to listen to reason.

*For those of you wondering, the multiverse is a geek term batted about by comic book aficionados and particle physicists alike. In a nutshell, different outcomes can produce different universes. For example, in universe A, an electron is a particle, while in universe B, the same electron is a wave of energy. In universe C, you read 50 Shades of Gray, while in universe D you read this wonderful, insightful book on the life of a teacher, and in universe E you hail the author of this book as one of the greatest writers of all time for his wit and charm. You get the picture.

1-29-2013
Tuesday

I apologize for taking so long to update the journal, but life does happen. With exam days, snow days, working on a fantasy novel, and trying to determine the best ways to deal with Caroline's aging parents, the inspirations just weren't flowing. So, I need to catch up on a few items.

My earth science kiddies did well on their exam. I can't discuss any particulars about it, but I was comforted when the majority of the class said it wasn't too bad. I only had three kids fail it: one can't speak English, and the other two quit trying the first week of school. So their performance doesn't surprise me. I will also have two zeros figured into the equation for the two kids who didn't show up for the exam, but that's just the way it is. When absences were not calculated into the equation, some teachers told their students not to show up on exam day. Now, they are figured into our final tally after a period of time has elapsed for adequate chances to make up the exam. In essence, now, when a kid doesn't show up for an exam, it's my fault.

Words can't express how proud I am of the little boogers. All of the begging, pleading, threatening, etc. paid off. One kid, who failed both semesters, came by my room today and hesitantly asked for his exam grade. It was at times like this that I love my job. I looked at a kid who had basically given-up, but who tried because I asked it of him, and I was able to tell him that not only did he make a C on the exam, but it was a high enough grade to enable him to pass the course. The look of relief, mixed with disbelief, combined with a healthy dash of joy radiating off of him, made the frustrations of the semester worth it. Thankfully, he didn't kiss me like a guy I taught many years ago did. I liked Sam, but not that much.

My school day is drastically different this semester. For starters, my average class size has dropped from 32 students to 28 students. It is amazing what a difference four or five students can make. Now, don't get me wrong. My fourth period last semester would have been a rough class if it only had twelve kids in it. Sometimes you get that kind of mix in a classroom. But, for the general classroom, the problems increase exponentially with each kid added above twenty-five. So, to only have twenty-eight kids in a class, feels like a breath of fresh air. I no longer feel like the head fish in a can of sardines. I can move around the room without tripping over someone. Even though I still long for the days when my largest class would have twenty-eight kids, I will enjoy the reprieve from overcrowding that is becoming all too typical in schools these days. It's sad really. If politicians would quit trying to place blame on everyone but themselves, and actually try to work with teachers and parents to fix the problems in schools (problems created by a lot of the misguided mandates and budget cuts) then my life would be a lot easier. One of the first areas they, the politicians, can address is the disgrace of overcrowded classes. If a kid comes from a problem home, the last thing that child needs is to packed into a classroom like a bunch of cattle in a feedlot.

The other major change in my day is my classes. This semester, I am teaching three Honors Chemistry classes. Overall, these are the best students Haversaw High has to offer. The best thing about them is that they understand, and get my jokes. Years ago, Sabrina, a girl in one of my regular level biology classes told me, "Mr. Gregory, I enjoyed your class. I never got any of your jokes, but you looked like you had fun telling them." I do have fun telling jokes, but it is even better when I get a response from a class. So, I'm enjoying myself.

My stress level dropped to near normal levels. (For the record, I'm still stressed about minor things such as job security, elimination of pension, will I ever see a pay increase, are my in-laws ready to move to an assisted living establishment, etc. You know, minor things.) June, a fellow teacher, remarked that she had not heard me yelling at a class. (For the record [again] the majority of times I yell at a class it is to simply get them to stop talking. Thirty-three kids talking at once have trouble hearing you when you meekly say, "Now, now, children. It would be in your best interest to desist from talking out of turn." You have to get their attention first, and boy, can I get their attention.) June was right. I have not had to yell at any of these classes. I walk into the room, conversation stops, and the students get out their materials for the day. This, more than anything, is why teachers tend to gravitate toward the honors level classes or the "better" schools. It's not that we don't want to help troubled kids. We do. It's not that we don't relish the idea of inspiring a group of kids to greatness. We do. But, when your day-to-day existence consists of having to yell at a group of kids to stop talking so you can actually take roll, let alone teach, your spirit gets ground to dust.

The idea of constantly fighting to get the majority of a class to write something down in the notebooks, to try to study for a test, and most importantly of all, to actually care, drains the soul of even the most devoted teacher. Students fail, schools fail. While bad teachers certainly exist, it has been my experience that the majority of time, it is not the fault of the men and women who strive to teach troubled kids. They are trying as hard as they can to make a difference. I know I have for the past semester, but you reach a point, when you simply can't take it anymore. So you either leave, or you become cynical. If anyone reading this doesn't think it will happen to them, I challenge that reader to try it. To date, no politician who belittles the teachers of "failing" schools or students has accepted my challenge.

1-30-2013
Wednesday

I had a conversation with a coworker today. Of course, I have conversations with coworkers every day, but this one was significant. Mrs. Grayson's, prediction for the future of education, based on the current political climate in North Carolina, is that high school as we know it will be gone within twenty years. The individual classroom where the teacher has interaction with the kids, where the teacher listens to the students, helps them with their problems, provides a sense of stability in this crazy world, will be gone. Instead, Mrs. Grayson's vision of the future classroom is one where over a hundred students are staring, glossy-eyed at a computer screen listening to earphones as a lackluster remote teacher or software program drones on and on with instruction. All compassion, all interaction, will be replaced by a digital, yet cost effective, program.

Only time will tell if her prediction is, indeed, a prophecy. My heartfelt prayer is that I hope she is wrong.

1-31-2013
Thursday

It's happened. I just read in the paper that a member of the General Assembly is going to introduce a bill that will arm teachers. In all fairness, it does not state that every teacher will be required to don their holsters with two six-shooters on their hips, but it is a start. To me, it is a dangerous start. I have heard it said that if you pull a gun on someone and you can't pull the trigger, then you are a greater threat to yourself, than to any attacker. I agree with the statement. I might as well hand over the gun, chest held high, and await my execution. I do not think I could pull that trigger and even if I could, my aim is so bad the assailant would be the safest person in the room. It is extremely possible that I would accidentally shoot the teacher in the next room who was safely behind a locked door.

The second situation that arouses my concerns is that if you arm the teachers, then what's next? Where will it end? Will kids be able to bring guns to school for their own protection? Will we have shootouts over funny looks?

In the American past, we've had our periods of lawlessness, where gun-toting vigilantes roamed the streets and roads, hunting down would be wrong doers and anyone who just happened to piss them off. I don't want to see that at Haversaw High. We're not trained to handle situations like this. How quickly could a standoff with an angry kid suddenly deteriorate into a situation that needs immediate armed action? Rumor, I am convinced travels faster than the speed of light. How quickly could a fight happen that rumor states involved a gun. Next, teachers are pulling their own guns out...Well, you get the picture.

I write this final argument against guns in the hands of teachers as a plea to understand the humanity of us all. We have to deal with a population that sometimes does not want to be at school. Society forces them to attend, but it doesn't enforce their behavior. You can't code that into a spreadsheet program. A lot of these kids fail and are bored as a result. So, they want to be entertained, and the teacher is both the source of their amusement and the focal point of their rage against the society that imprisons them within the walls of learning. (Think about that horse you've been told about that you can lead to water.) I, as well as many of my coworkers, have been pushed to the brink where sanity is lost. Anything could happen. I am happy to say that no one that I know has crossed the line of appropriate and inappropriate responses, but we've all been pretty close. Most leave the room for a few minutes to calm down. Before you pass judgment on us, I would ask how many of my readers have had a student screaming at them because he did not prepare a lab the day before because his wife had suffered a miscarriage. I have. Now, throw a gun into that equation, and a kid who is out of control in the classroom. Maybe, you will see why teachers should never have guns in the classroom.

Writers note: It's basically the same reason why psychotic nut-cases should not be allowed access to thirty-round clips and assault style rifles.

On a lighter note, if you want to have some fun, try calculating how much of a year you can hold your breath. It's merry-making at its best, and is a good exercise in conversions, a skill essential in chemistry. I also tell the kids that it's a good way to impress girls at a party. Imagine, you see a cute girl standing near the punchbowl, and you want to talk to her, but you don't know where to start. Do you attempt bold and daring, or a lower key approach with "Sup?" (After exhaustive research, I have found that the form of greeting "Sup?" can roughly be translated as "Excuse me kind sir/miss, might I enquire as to how your day has been thus far?"). I advice the guys to walk up to the cute girl and say, "Hi, did you know I can hold my breath for 1.46 x 10-6 years? It sounds mysterious and manly. Little will she suspect that you really said you could hold your breath for 46 seconds.

I do warn the kids, however, to avoid idiot mistakes. In conversions, it is real easy to mess up your conversion factor. The results can be quite humorous. I had one student last year tell me he could hold his breath for 300,000 years.

2-4-2013
Monday

I had a first today. I was called to assist in the random drug test. I'll resist the temptation for a cheap pun and not say that I was pissed over the situation. It turns out that we were shorthanded (our tallest assistant principal [that was another pun, in case you missed it] was out due to the sudden death of his mother. So, they needed an able body, i.e. anybody with first period planning (although I will pretend it was for my wit and charm) to help pass out paperwork, direct the kids to the proper location, and make sure no unauthorized person goes into the bathroom. I will say, I was very much relieved (another cheap pun) that I was not required to monitor the bathroom.

Confidentiality forbids me from discussing anything else that occurred during the drug testing, although I will state that it was an easy assignment and pretty boring, but if you want to envision me chasing after a young delinquent who, after refusing to take the test, made a break for freedom and I was forced to hunt him down in the streets of NYC, please go ahead. I did, however, have time to think, which could be a dangerous thing. The random testing is the chief component of a program required of all students who participate in an extracurricular activity. I will not address the legality of this concept other than to say I will have no problems when my daughters will have to participate in it.

I did consider that these kids are not that much different from kids when I was in high school way back when phones were still attached to the walls. Drugs were a problem in the 1980s and they are a problem in 2013. When I was in high school, people chose to turn a blind eye to the issue. Drugs were only in the inner city. Small town NC would never have to face such issues. Well, let me tell you, apparently I got lost on my way to a few parties and wound up in the ghettos of Philadelphia. Needless to say, there was a drug problem at my old alma mater. There is a drug problem at Haversaw High, and there is a drug problem at (insert name) high school in any part of the country. The drugs are present, and the kids are using them.

This also highlights a common theme I've griped about for years. These kids aren't little babies anymore. They are making adult decisions, sometimes choosing wisely and sometimes choosing poorly, and they should be treated as adults. We, as parents, do the students a severe injustice when we treat them as children who need to be protected from every little challenge, especially from the mean, old, teachers at Haversaw High. Parents, please let your child be wrong, to learn that there are consequences for their decisions. I would much rather my child learn this lesson for something trivial such as throwing someone else's jacket on the roof of the ticket booth at the football stadium than when they are confronted with the choice to use an illegal substance or not. For the record, the jacket incident happened last year on a nature walk with one of my earth/environmental science classes. The boy was sent to the office for disciplinary action as well as to protect him from having the snot beat out of him. The owner of the jacket was a good bit bigger than he was. After procuring a ladder, risking life-and-limb climbing to the top of the building, and finally rescuing the $80 Abercrombie and Fitch jacket, which bore a strong resemblance to the $20 hoodie I saw at Walmart, I was in no mood for the phone call that followed where the parents tried to justify their son's actions. My mother would have beaten me into the next week and then made me buy the other kid a new jacket. As I said earlier, if any parents are reading this, please do not cover up for your child's mistakes. It is by making mistakes that we grow into maturity.

2-7-2013
Thursday

I've been out of school for a couple of days. Mckenzie, my older daughter, has had a pretty nasty case of something. We know for certain that she has a sinus infection, which has been kicking her asthma's figurative butt. Now it appears that it was possibly a mycoplasma form of pneumonia, which was wrecking havoc with her lungs. So, my focus on life has not been school. Throwing together lesson plans sums up my contribution to the educational process for the past few days. I guess I've been a drain on the public coffers, putting an extreme burden on the good taxpayers of North Carolina. To all of my fellow North Carolinians, I want to offer my heartfelt apologies. Actually, the average taxpayer understands the reality that teachers are also parents. Sometimes, our elected officials lack that foresight. So it is to the elected officials, the news media, and to anyone else who feels that teachers are machines whose sole purpose is to train the future generation, machines without families or feelings, that I offer my apologies.

As a result I've been out of the loop, so to speak, of current happenings at Haversaw High. So I was surprised when I walked into Sandy's room to see her break down into tears. Sandy and I have been friends for years. She's a damn good teacher, one of the best at Haversaw. At times like this, I have found that simply showing support is the best course of action. I'm not a touchy-feely type of person, so I just sat down and talked. Sandy didn't want to rehash an ongoing problem, (I wouldn't share it in this narrative even if she had) but she seemed to appreciate the gesture. She wanted me to tell her something funny, but I'm drained. I recognize her greater issue. Regardless of the primary cause of her distress, the underlying issue is one facing all teachers across vast areas of the country. We're cracking. More and more expectations have been heaped upon us. We're supposed to play the role of compassionate nurturer while maintaining a high degree of academic rigor while personally ensuring every student graduates. To inspire the best minds to accomplish this task, various public figures have referred to teachers as parasites sucking the public coffers dry, we're blamed for failing schools, our resources have been cut so our classrooms are overcrowded with woefully outdated teaching material, our pay has been stagnant for years, and the General Assembly wants to cut our benefits. Maybe I'm crazy, but I don't quite see how this is going to work.

So, I'm out of funny ideas to help Sandy. No cute anecdote or humorous example of antics from long ago will make it any better. Nothing will change the fact that the powers-that-be have turned something that used to be fun, into a living hell. Years ago, I loved going to work. It was fun. Sure I had some classes that made me want to jump into a cage full of hyper Chihuahuas, but I loved teaching. Now, I'm walking into classrooms only to see good friends reduced to tears, and there's nothing I can do to help.

2-10-2013
Sunday

Have you ever wondered what it is like to play the prelude in a handbell choir during the Sunday worship service at church, and then have to run out of the sanctuary to vomit? Thankfully, our associate pastor is a bit long-winded, so I was able to make it back to my place before we started playing the offertory. Which, despite the nausea and the taste of bile, I was able to nail. Now that's a performance, or an answered prayer that I didn't toss my cookies in the low C bell, which was more than capable of holding the volume; however, I'm sure our choir director would not have wanted to put it to the test. If you were wondering, it was not a pleasant experience. I spent the rest of the day in bed and I don't think I need to say, that I am not going to school tomorrow. Norovirus is a real pain in the....

2-12-2013
Tuesday

Going back to school after an absence is never fun, especially when the absence was due to a stomach illness. Schools are comprised of sights and sounds that normally reside in the back-

85

ground spaces of your mind. They are absorbed and quickly filed under the heading of "school" in your mind's file cabinet. However, add nausea to the equation, and it's a whole new game. Simply walking into the bathroom is a challenge with the goal of the game being, "Let's see if I can do this and not vomit." The normal background aroma of funky locker mixed with cheap cologne combined with the ever fragrant smell emanating from the AC system hits you at subconscious levels which skip the higher parts of the brain and moves directly to the gag reflex of the animal trying to determine if the gooey stuff on the ground is edible or not. Needless to say, it has not been a pleasant morning. At least my sub report was good and I have not received any parent complaints.

It's amazing some of the complaints I have received over the years. I had a parent complain one year of my choice of a substitute teacher when I was out on paternity leave. The mother's concern (I use the word concern very loosely because I'm trying to make this a G-rated diary. When I received the e-mail, I used a lot harsher terms.) was that the person covering my class for my week leave was not adequately knowledgeable in the realms of biology. The person in question was working on his doctoral thesis in neurobiology. The real issue was that her son failed a quiz under Mr. Jay's care. Obviously, her son was nearly perfect in every way, so it had to be either my fault for wanting to take time off for the birth of Mckenzie, or it was Mr. Jay's fault. My wife was also blasted for her sub while she was out on maternity leave.

The worst case though happened to Sandy. She had to miss almost a week of school when her father suffered a massive stroke. A student screamed at Sandy upon her return for her expectation that the students should work while she was away. The parents were mortified, but the damage was done. My take on the whole affair was that either the kid was a total jerk, or the parents had been egging it on at home, and the kid then took matters into his own hands. Who knows, I just work here.

I just wish that parents, students, and everyone else would realize that teachers are humans, and things happen. In the course of a week, Mckenzie had been diagnosed with pneumonia and I puked my guts out. I didn't plan any of this, but it happened. In two weeks, I will have to miss another day when Caroline has some minor surgery. Just because I work in a school, doesn't mean life quits hurtling its little ups-and-downs at my family. Parents need to understand that we do the best we can.

Now, if a teacher is out and is a jerk about it, then that is another situation. However, most teachers try to catch their students up as best as they can. So, if we have to miss multiple days for illness, family illness, birth of a child, or even for a trip (although to be realistic, with two months off in the summer, the trip had better be short), please accept the situation and have your child deal with the circumstances. Most teachers are more than happy to stay after school or spend extra time in class (if course curriculum dictated by state and federal governments allow) to help your child recover from the missed work. But, ultimately, if the teacher left adequate plans for their absence, then it is the responsibility of the child to step up to the proverbial plate and do what is needed for their grade. While I am a firm advocate that nothing beats a living, breathing teacher for learning, sometimes, it is okay for a student to learn something on his or her own.

(Day of Gloom or Is it?)
2-13-2013
Wednesday

The day started with me receiving my first cussing out in almost six years. Every other word began with the letter "f" and ended with the letter "k", although, to be fair, a few ended with "king." I'll let you fill in the missing two letters. To make matters worse, it wasn't even my kid administering the tongue-lashing. I was just helping out a fellow teacher whose student refused to stop and recognize a gesture of good will. A simple, "Why yes, I am so sorry. It was incredibly rude of me to walk off while you were trying to figure out why I was acting like such a prude," would have stopped any further disciplinary actions. We all understand that sometimes, you just have a lousy day. Sometimes you do something stupid. Most of the times, if a student stops and explains his actions, then we, the teachers, will fluff it off as long as they calm down in the process.

Unfortunately, John didn't see it that way. He took the approach of "I'm in trouble, so I might as well do it right." It's a shame. I found out later after escorting John and his mouth to the office, that he had already gotten in trouble earlier that morning. He was angry, an understandable response. However, instead of informing his teacher or me of the situation, he decided to go for broke. That decision cost him an additional six days of suspension.

That was the start of my day. "How could things get worse?" I asked myself. The answer came a few hours later. As you have probably guessed, I'm an aspiring writer. A few hours later, I found out that my novel-length, contemporary fiction manuscript was knocked out of a major writing contest in the first round. I'll add that to my list of rejections. It's a tough business to break into. A fact that I can understand. I just wish I could get some professional to read the blasted thing.

As is often the case in the teaching profession, it was the students who bailed me out of my gloom. We were studying molar mass conversions in chemistry. This is where you take chemistry from the mass level, where we live, to the molecular level, where chemistry happens. The conversion itself is fairly easy, although the kids will tend to make it difficult. To accomplish this conversion, you take the average atomic mass of an element from the periodic table of elements, do a little bit of chemistry magic to convert atomic mass units into grams/mole, and do a calculation. It's both exciting and useful. Moles, the unit of measurement for the amount of a substance, not the little fuzzy critters who are tearing up my yard, are what you see when you read a chemical formula or balance an equation. To add further excitement to the mix, you can multiply the moles of a substance by a number derived by some Italian guy almost a hundred years ago, and you have the number of atoms found in a substance. See, chemistry is pretty cool no matter what the masses say. (Sorry about that last pun) Today the students applied this knowledge to real samples of metals. They did so well at this that I simply sat back and watched, answering the odd question here-and-there. After more rejections for my novel than I care to count, it was nice to see that I could do something right. I may not make it as an author (although if whoever is reading this would like to disagree, I would more than appreciate it), but I'm a damn good teacher!

6

"The Day of Love"

2-14-2013
Thursday

I won the prize for "Best Valentines' Gift by a Husband" today. Actually, the foundation for this gift was delivered a few days ago with a single act. For the past seventy-two hours, this nugget has been circulating, working its magic upon my wife, setting her up for my ultimate gift of…saltines and water. I'm going to interpret her loving response of "hruuuggggh" to mean, "My dearest husband, what did I ever do to deserve a man such as you? My heart melts with the thought of your loving gift, I will cherish it always, or at least until I throw it up in a little while." This is not panning out to be the most romantic of days in the Gregory household.

On a lighter note, I had a McDonald's Angus Mushroom and Swiss burger last night, the first time I had felt hungry since Saturday. One bite into its juicy goodness, and the lively rhythms of Jimmy Buffet's "Cheeseburger in Paradise" began ringing in my ears. The first real meal after a particularly bad stomach bug is indeed, a little bit of paradise.

However, my younger daughter was still able to get into the mood of things, even though the most important person in the world in her eyes was incapacitated. She placed a homemade heart in the box of Pop Tarts as a special Valentines' gift for me. I found it after she innocently asked for a Pop Tart for breakfast. It was sweet. I'm going to put it up on my bulletin board when I get to school.

The day was relatively uneventful, for a Valentines' Day. In years past, Valentines' Day has meant chaos personified. This year, however, I only had one giant, pink teddy bear delivered to my room by a would-be-lover. Other than the normal classroom antics of jumping onto a table screaming "It's Harry Styles!"* at the top of my lungs to simulate an electron absorbing energy and entering the excited state where it leaps to the next energy level in an atom all while being observed by my assistant principal who, I am fairly certain thinks I'm certifiably insane, the day was downright boring. I do want to give a hearty thanks to the PTA Moms for the wonderful Bar-B-Cue** lunch they provided.

The only sour note, other than my wife's illness, occurred when I complemented our secretary for her daughter's boyfriend. I taught Fred. He's a knucklehead, but seemed like a good kid. He met his girlfriend at the door to the school office with a big stuffed dog, and a bouquet of flowers. Jennifer and I watched the whole ordeal. I thought it was cute. Both of them are freshmen. While we made fun of them in that special way adults save for young lovers, it was sweet. However, I found out as the temperature in the office dropped to near absolute zero when I mentioned it to our secretary, she did not like it and is opposed to her daughter dating at all. I still think it was cute, but ask me again when it's Kaitlyn or Mckenzie getting the gift. I may change my mind by then.

*For those of you over the age of fifteen, Harry Styles is a singer in the boy band known as One Direction. Harry is following a long line of teen heartthrobs dating back to at least the late Renaissance. Think life-sized posters, preteen girls pledging their undying love, and daughters (and possibly their mothers as well) screaming at the top of their lungs whenever he walks on stage, and you've got the image. I used to use Justin Bieber, but the Beiberfever as faded in the minds of the teen set.

**If you are not from the South, you probably have no clue as to what type of meal our PTA Moms provided. In the South, Bar-B-Cue is a noun meaning roast pork that has been pulled and chopped. Some experts disagree how exactly to prepare it, but the basic roast pork is universally agreed as the key ingredient, unless you're in Texas. At this point, Bar-B-Cue includes beef.

I found out last night I'm in the wrong line of work. We're having work done on our house, and last night we received the initial estimate. Let's just say I'm suffering from a wee bit of sticker shock. Thankfully we have some money put back from a life insurance policy from my grandmother. The work really needs to be done, and I hate painting. I'm excited about it, but the price was a bit of surprise. I'm not certain how much these guys want to make an hour, but I think it is safe to say that it exceeds what I earn.

Speaking of work, I've run into an age-old problem. (At least as age-old as the Internet.) Teachers are required to obtain fifteen renewal credits every five years in order to renew their teaching certificate. Normally, this is not a problem because the system offered plenty of opportunities to obtain these credits in the past. Five years ago, staff development funds were slashed. Apparently providing the training that the state deemed was necessary to keep teachers at the peak of their teaching abilities was considered unnecessary and wasteful spending. I understand this problem, and given the choice, I agree with the Haversaw system in eliminating staff development funds to keep teachers in the classroom. But, it's bloody annoying now that I'm up against the wall trying to find staff development so I can keep my license.

In my case, the situation is particularly annoying because the state designated certain types of credit a teacher must obtain for recertification. I have completed everything except 0.4 credits of technology. One hour of workshop time equates to 0.1 credits. So I need a class, or combination of classes that combine for four hours of instruction. All of Haversaw's technology workshops offered at this time are on-line. Some face-to-face classes are provided at a later date, but I don't want to wait until the last minute on my credits. Online technology courses sound great until you consider the implications of this. I'm a technology klutz. Anything silicon based, with the exception of silicon dioxide (that's quartz for you non-geologists), immediately stops working when I touch it. Several years ago, I had the pleasure of teaching in a trailer, or "Mobile Educational Facility" as I liked to call the piece of junk. Outside of the twenty-odd leaks that were apparent anytime it rained and the mice, it was a pleasant experience if you are comparing it to a stay on a deserted island with no food or water, that is infested with any manner of creepy-crawly things. The highlight of the trailer was my wireless system. I personally thought the system was haunted because it would often lose its signals when the buses pulled into the school. Our tech person wouldn't believe me on the bus issue until I made him come out to my Mobile Education Facility at 3:15 when the yellow-hued monstrosities arrived. Right on cue the signal went out. In fact, the only time the signal was great for my system was when they mowed the grass. The tech people are still trying to figure that one out.

So the idea of my taking an on-line course to learn how to use on-line technology is laughable at best. After haggling with the on-line registration menu yesterday, I finally received my notification that I could begin my course, only to find out that the system didn't like my password. Please note that this is the same password I use for all of the logins at Haversaw. Everything else likes it, but apparently the on-line forum thinks my password has cooties. I'm beginning to think I should receive my credit if I can ever log onto the silly thing.

2-20-2013

Wednesday

I'm still waiting for word from our technology help desk, which you need a computer programming degree to navigate, as to when they will have my login issue fixed. I understand that my emergency isn't necessarily their emergency, but I really need to get moving with this on-line Moodle thing. (I'm not certain where the word Moodle originated, but I can state that my word processor does not recognize it. I think it is either a cute way of saying module or a hungry Italian with a speech impediment created it.)

Another issue arose today which highlighted the fact that just because you can say something, doesn't mean that you should. My wife sent me an email stating that she's been exposed to pertussis. So she has to go to the doctor and get a precautionary prescription for a Z-pac. Over the years we've seen a rise in cases of diseases we once sought safely contained. Laws were in place. If you weren't vaccinated, then you didn't attend school until you could prove that you had obtained the necessary shots. Thus, the safety of the rest of the school was ensured.

Around ten years ago, a celebrity made it her goal in life to point out the evils of vaccinations. Citing dubious and long-since-discredited scientific research, this person urged her viewers to be wary of vaccines because of the potential link with autism. Please do not get me wrong. My heart goes out to anyone trying to raise an autistic child. But the simple fact remains that every credible scientific and medical study has found absolutely no risk of developing autism from a vaccine. Yet, because of the actions of this celebrity with no medical knowledge, we've had droves of parents suddenly developing a religious intolerance to vaccines. Ironically, these same parents lose their religious inhibitions when it comes to antibiotics. So now my family has been placed at risk because someone else decided that the fictitious link was more dangerous than the very real risk of developing a potentially life-threatening disease.

2-21-2013
Thursday

One day I'm going to learn that, when I see an editorial in the paper that has the words teacher-learning nexus in the title, I really shouldn't read it. Apparently I've been tackling the art of teaching wrong for the past twenty-years. Not only have I been mistaken in my approach, but so were Socrates and Plato. Who knew that no real learning has occurred in human history until the advent of a specific computer-based education system? Wow! The Greek philosophers, the Chinese wise men, the Renaissance, the builders of the Industrial Revolution, and, dare I say, the people who created computers, were all a fluke. Who knew? According to the author of this editorial, true learning occurs when you can individualize instruction with a computer program.

Let's consider this concept of individualizing instruction with a computer program. While, yes, students can work at their own pace, the computer is still hampered by its programming. Can the computer see the look of confusion in a young man's eye when he is confronted with the idea of how the average atomic mass can also equal the molar mass of an element? Can the computer spontaneously create a goofy catchphrase to help the student memorize the correct order of for a complex list such as the Hierarchy of Names in biological classifications? The answer to these questions is an emphatic NO!

The computer can only do what the programmer had the foresight to anticipate. I can tell you from personal experience that, no matter how you try to idiot proof something, your students will always exceed your wildest expectations. Trust me, I've been plowing my way through the "individualized" Moodle for my tech credit, and I'm clueless as to the author's purpose.

Is learning in a classroom restricted to the mere mastering of a discipline? What about the social aspects where students learn from a mentor what it means to be an adult? Can a computer offer sympathy for the girl who is in tears because of a nasty breakup where her former boyfriend is now spreading tales of what an easy lay she was? Can the computer look at those tear-filled eyes and realize that the Quantum Mechanical Model of an Atom can wait for a few minutes? Can you envision a computer standing out in the hallway with the young girl as she breaks down into sobs, unable to focus because of the fury she is experiencing from parents at home as a result of the slander that they believe is true?

Once again the answer is an emphatic NO!

Teaching is so much more than the learning of facts. It is the interactions, the compassion, the love a teacher holds for his/her students that takes the raw material of students and turns them into adults. Unlike an automobile assembly line, you can't screw in a few bolts and weld a few seams to accomplish the goal of creating a well-rounded adult. It takes human interaction and no computer can do this.

My day ended on a personal sad note. As I was walking out the door I learned that Sandy, a dear friend and someone I've worked with for over a decade, is more than likely leaving Haversaw High at the end of the year. I've expected this day would come ever since her daughter was born nearly nine years ago. Sandy lives on the opposite end of the county, and family commitments have been pulling her away from Haversaw ever since her child was born. I understand all of this, but it still doesn't mean I have to like it. While the job will not be definite until the teacher allotments are computed in May, when a department chair calls, it's a pretty good chance the position will be open. In my twenty-year career, I have had to say goodbye far too often. It sucks.

On a much more humorous note, it's 7:41 p.m. on a Thursday night, they are forecasting a potential for icing tomorrow, but the temperature is currently 44 degrees with partially cloudy skies. The system just canceled school for tomorrow. Go figure.

2-25-2013
Monday (aka The Blahs)

It's shaping up to be one of those days. I have to deal with psycho-mom at school, I'm tired of the cold weather, someone has been sick in our house for the entire month of February, my stomach is still not right, it's Monday, and I could easily just roll over and go back to sleep. Unfortunately, calling in sick because I don't want to be in charge for the day is not an option. I know I'm whining, but sometimes you just need to get it out of your system. So I'm going to plow ahead and be the teacher today, but I'm not going to be happy about it.

My first deed for the day was to talk to an administrator. If you have never dealt with a psycho-mom, then you've lived a blessed life. A psycho-mom is someone who really needs to find a job other than harassing teachers. This semester I may have the winner for craziest mother of the year. Her child is failing and, of course, every ounce of the blame is mine. If I'm doing something wrong and a parent wants to confront me, then that's okay. A parent is their child's most important advocate. I've had to be "That Parent" on a few occasions for my own kids. However, when it is my fault that a child is failing chemistry when the same child refuses to do any homework, never takes notes in class, will half-heartedly work on an assignment, and generally acts like a royal pain, then I have issues. I know parents love their kids, but sometimes your kid is a jackass and his/her actions will have consequences.

This is a plea to psycho-moms everywhere. Instead of sitting on the computer waiting to pounce the second that a failing grade is entered into the computer, talk to your child and explain that ultimately he/she is the one responsible. While my job is to teach the material, I cannot force the students to write that information down. And I certainly cannot go to their houses and hold their hands while they attempt the homework. That is the job of the parent.

Homework is not a cruel and unusual punishment; it is an exercise to reinforce the concepts taught in class. This stuff isn't easy. Parents please understand that, sometimes, your child will struggle. This is part of the growing process. You cannot mature into an adult without having to work through a few things. Instead, psycho-mom sits by the computer waiting for a new grade to be entered into our grading database. Once I post the grade, the parents can access it so they can monitor their child's progress.

I spent the last part of my planning period entering grades. The kid failed a quiz. Before I could run to the bathroom, psycho-mom fired off an email demanding to know why her son/daughter failed the molar mass quiz, and then fired another email to the principal when I did not respond in a timely manner. For the record, the email arrived right at the beginning of second period, and I do teach for that entire class period. I was going to answer it at the end of the day when I can sit down, instead of telling thirty kids that I have to stop class to answer an email from a parent who should really be out doing something productive with her life instead of making mine miserable.

As I said, it's one of those days. On a final note, I just checked the forecast for tonight. We have rain with a low of 36 degrees. I wonder if we're going to have school on Tuesday.

2-26-2013
Tuesday

We did go to school today. A lot of people griped, but as far as I could tell, while I was stuck in traffic trying to get my daughter and her friend to their school, the roads were wet. Yes, ice formed on the trees, but I do not think the roads were icy for the majority of Haversaw County. On Friday, the system justifiably caught flak for canceling school. "The roads were fine!" people yelled. "This was stupid!" they cried. "We're raising a bunch of wimps!" others said.

Today, however, when the temperatures were above freezing at ground level and the roads were clear, albeit wet, people were screaming again. "You're putting our children at risk!" people yelled. "The roads were treacherous," people cried. "This was stupid," they said.

The two calls exemplified the adage, "Damned if you do, and damned if you don't." Two similar weather conditions, (although for the record, I think there was some ice accumulation last Friday) two different calls, and the same result of public outcry. I feel sorry for the people who have to make those decisions. For my part, because my painter wants to start work tomorrow, I could have really used a day off to take down pictures, store valuables, etc.

On a different note, my students worked diligently on an assignment learning about the marvelous trends of the periodic table (Essential Standard Chm 1.3, Clarifying Objectives Chm.1.3.2 and Chm.1.3.3). It's such a pleasant change not to have to scream at the kids to get them to work.

2-27-2013
Wednesday

Will February Ever End?

I've heard this question posed in many different formats. Why, as February is the shortest month in the calendar, does it seem to take forever to end? I share this lament. I've chronicled our medical ills this month. Now, we're looking at the possibility that Caroline may have a bulging/herniated disk.

This brings up an interesting question. In the rhetoric by various public figures and blogs, teachers have gone from being servants of the people to being leeches sucking the blood of the public coffers dry. Interesting choice of words, that for some strange reason, most teachers find offensive. Let's take a look at how Caroline and I are sucking the coffers dry. While we are remodeling our house, it is eleven years old and still has the original carpet and paint, which is in a sad state. The only reason we can afford this now is the timely arrival of a payment from a life insurance policy held by my grandmother.

Our take-home pay has been stagnant for years and the guar-antied bonus for high performance (which a quick check of the blogs indicates that the groups who believe teachers are leaches are demanding) hasn't been paid in years. Haversaw has ranked at the highest level for the past five years running, and we haven't received one single dime of our state-mandated "merit pay." Yep, I'm draining those public coffers dry. By a rough estimate, the state of NC owes me nearly $10,000 of bonus pay that I will never see. So, please excuse me if I'm a little doubtful as to how well the merit-based pay system is going to work.

Last night, the pain in my wife's back was excruciating. It was so bad that both of us considered a trip to the emergency room. However, our cushy government benefits package has a $200 co-pay plus 20% of the bill for emergency room visits. It costs $75 dollars to visit urgent care, and a specialist visit costs us $70 just to walk into the office. With after school care, dance, gymnastics, and lessons for viola (Mckenzie) and piano (Kaitlyn) our budget is stretched to the limit. Based on the costs of Caroline's surgery last year for an accidental injury, medical expenses can be crip-pling. Mckenzie has asthma. It cost me over $60 to simply fill her albuterol prescription, a life-saving medication. I'm draining the public coffers to the point that I'm thanking God that my grand-mother was able to leave us money. So, we'll be all right.

I understand that times are tough, but please don't blast the public servants who are servants, not slaves. A servant enters into a salary agreement with the master for services rendered. That's what teachers, police officers, firefighters, etc. have done. Please don't blast us when we actually expect the master to honor the contract he signed.

On a different note, we had a threat of a possible shooting at school. For those of you who bemoan the fact that teachers, po-lice, etc. can retire at an early age I have one question. When was the last time you were expected to lay down your life for the people under your care? I'm expected to do just that every day I walk through the doors of Haversaw High. It's an expectation

I will keep if it comes to pass. I hope that puts a little bit of light into the benefit of letting us retire after thirty years of service to the state and your children.

I am a public servant and damn proud of it.

Updates

Rumor is a nasty child of our technological society. While I cannot state what the real reason for our lockdown was, a situation occurred last night and was properly dealt with in an appropriate manner. Everything should have been fine. Instead, rumor spread like wildfire. From a statement tantamount to "I'm bringing gum to school" it turned into "Someone is bringing a gun to school" to "Bob and Bill are going on a shooting rampage tomorrow." The rumors even targeted a group of students that apparently had no connection with the original cause. As is usually the case, this particular group was comprised of kids who were a little on the odd side, a prime target for a crowd of panicked people in need of a scapegoat.

Parents panicked, social media went wild, and it was rumored that police had ransacked three homes and found a cache of weapons that could have armed a small army. Ironically, in the faculty meeting we had for the discussion of the situation, the police said they had tracked down every possible rumor and all of them were groundless. During my three classes, I had a total of 38 kids. By the end of the day, I had one student tell me that her sister in Chapel Hill sent a text asking if it was true that a student had been gunned down at Haversaw. The funny thing is Haversaw High was the safest place to be today. We had more police present than we had students.

On the home front, Caroline's back has several severely pulled muscles. Our doctor, who we now have to pay a $30 co-pay plus 20% after the deductible has been met, prescribed her medications that promise to send her to La-La Land. She's going to be out for the next two days. While she is still hurting, at least she is improving. Which is good , because she flies out in two days to present at her first national AP Calculus workshop in NYC.

3-3-2013
Sunday

We got Caroline back safe and sound. She got to La Guardia early enough for her flight that she then managed to arrange an earlier flight out. So she reached Piedmont-Triad International Airport in Greensboro well ahead of schedule. We were all pleased and happy that her back had survived the trip and was now in better shape than when she left.

Caroline had a great experience and played the role of ambassador for her school well. I hope her administration is pleased. While the administration's pleasure at a teacher representing the school on the national level should be a given, it isn't always the case. Years ago, a friend of mine was selected to present a workshop at The National Science Teacher Association conference. It was a great honor. The administration could only see that my friend required a substitute teacher for two days. They were lukewarm, at best, with the praise that should have been delivered in copious amounts. My friend was furious, an emotion that marred what should have been a great memory of a job well done.

In an effort to show how skewed our society has become, last year I had to cover the class of a coach who missed school for an athletics meeting attended by all but one of Haversaw's principals and most of the coaches. The meeting was to honor the achievements of one of our coaches. I relate this story, not to belittle the feats of our athletes and their coaches, but to point out that my friend was all but criticized for missing school for the opportunity to influence science education across the nation.

For athletics though, we rearranged numerous teachers' schedules so the coaches and principals could attend a system-wide meeting.

3-5-2013
Tuesday
ACT Day

In our unrelenting drive to hold teachers, and students, to a limited degree, accountable, Haversaw High is giving the ACT to all juniors today. This test was either mandated or chosen by the state government (I never have been able to figure out which is true) as our national-level exam for continued funding of the Race to The Top Incentive. We took the money and now we have to play by the federal government's rules, and that means we have to give a national-level exam as one of our benchmarks for success. I'm okay with this concept. The problem occurs when you factor into the account that we're still playing by our own rules as well. So we test the kids out the wazoo. Today, we're basically spending all day giving the ACT, four plus hours of testing, lunch, and then less than an hour each for the two afternoon classes. We did the same thing for the PLAN test, which is a pre-ACT test, last semester for the sophomores. Both tests required over an hour of additional time to fill out administrative paperwork. Last semester, exams spanned eight days on account of Common Exams and state End-of-Course tests or EOCs. It looks like the spring semester will bring ten days of exams. Considering that in the past, we gave two exams a day, which would have created a four-day exam schedule for Haversaw High, the mandated testing has removed fourteen days of instructional time from our calendar. Because the South still views the SAT as two steps below the Trinity in importance, we will spend another day giving the Pre-SAT to our sophomores as well. Now, we're up to fifteen days spent testing during this semester alone. That is a lot of instructional time eliminated for tests that, in essence, measures how well I am doing as a teacher.

All griping aside, sometimes you just have to be a little silly. My job for this morning's test was to yell at the kids (I'm sorry, speak in an encouraging voice for them to have their photo IDs ready) as they walked into the hallway where the tests were administrated. I assumed the role of airport security. After informing them to please have their identification ready and to secure their phones, I began to tell them to proceed in an orderly manner to the security checkpoint and to remove all metal objects and their shoes. One boy was carrying a box of Girl Scout cookies, which I informed him to hand them to the waiting teachers, who would make sure they were stored in a safe location after ensuring they were non-hazardous. My presentation was particularly effective, though, when I stood in front of the restroom so my already loud voice was amplified by the room's echo effect. I was impressed. I lost my composure and burst into laughter when I envisioned myself at Disney World giving directions to "please remain seated and to keep your arms and hands within the ride vehicle at all times." I thought I was crazy until our testing coordinator said we should all starting dancing to "YMCA" by the Village People. I wonder how they would code a testing misadministration for the faculty line dancing in the hallway. These tests are stressful for teachers, so sometimes you have to act up.

3-6-2013
Wednesday

It's never a good sign when a friend has to pause in her phone conversation to vomit. That's what happened to Caroline last night. Norovirus is running rampart through Haversaw County, and Caroline's coworker fell victim to its evil influence. In case you have never experienced noro's loving embrace, it starts with the joys of vomiting, followed by the ecstasy of diarrhea, and finishes with the pleasure of intense intestinal cramping. Needless to say, Caroline's friend was not going to school today. Caroline willingly agreed to get everything in order, including acting as a substitute coach for her school's equivalent of Quiz Bowl. It'll create a late night for Caroline, but it's always nice to help a friend.

3-7-2013
Thursday

Rene Descartes said, "I think, therefore I am." Todays meeting inspired me to alter the great philosopher's quote to "I sign papers, therefore I am." I'm a member of what was once known as the SAT committee or the Student Assistance Team Committee. It has since been changed to IST. To be perfectly honest, I don't know what the official name is. I believe it may be Individualized Support Team, but don't quote me on this particular issue. Acronyms tend to change with each new administration in Capital City, so I gave up keeping track of them a long time ago. The core mission is the same, regardless of the name. We're the first line for parents seeking special services for their child. Of course, the parents may view us as the first hurdle they have to pass to get those services.

The specifics of the meeting this morning are irrelevant for this discussion, and it would be illegal for me to release the details anyway. What struck me, though, was the sheer volume of paperwork required for each student. We had to keep minutes of the meeting, which everyone present had to sign, just in case somebody decided to question the contents of the meeting at a later date. We had to sign a report on the modifications implemented for the student after an earlier meeting. After participating in a sick parody of taking a bottle of some non-alcoholic substance off the wall and passing it around, except it was the modification form, our committee chair, realized we had missed a form. So, we repeated the procedure with the new form. Next, came the final form exiting the student from the care of IST and passing her along to exceptional services, which is the current incarnation of special education. The poor kid had a file measured in inches. That's a lot of signatures. The sad thing is every one of those stages of signatures has, at some time, been questioned in a court of law. As a result, every single stage of the exceptional children's process has to be verified and verified again with multiple signatures to protect the school, and if the truth be told, the student as well.

3-13-2013
Wednesday

I talked to Mr. Flair today and I'm happy to report that I have apparently not pissed him off yet. That's an accomplishment for me. With Mr. Peace, our former principal, it seemed like all I had to do was burp and fart at the same time, and I was in his office. One of the best instances involved a kid who had embellished a diagram of Torricelli's barometer, an inverted tube inserted into a dish of mercury. I won't go into minute details, but I will say that the boy's diagram involved hair and a squirting fountain on top. The kid's mother saw the diagram in his notes, and confronted her son. In the grand tradition of students everywhere, his defense was, "I drew exactly what Mr. Gregory put on the board." When the mother called the office, I was summoned to appear before Mr. Peace, because obviously I was guilty. In Mr. Peace's defense, he relented when I showed him the actual diagram.

So, by March, the failure to be summoned to Mr. Flair' office, coupled with a pleasant conversation, was a breath of fresh air compared to the past seven years. Still, I can't tell what type of principal he will prove to be. He's experienced and holds himself with the bearing of one who has weathered a storm or two. But his communication is somewhat lacking. We have been left floundering many times during the course of the year, trying to determine how to implement a procedure or mandate. However, with discipline, he is quick to administer justice. A possible clue to his psyche came in a comment he made during our conversation.

"If something isn't a problem, why make it one?" he asked in response to a clarifying question I had posed concerning dress code.

It may be that his philosophy is to lie low until he's needed. Only time will tell how this will play out with Haversaw's population and their parents.

3-14-2013
Thursday

I've decided that I'm insane. It's okay, though, I'm the harmless type that peacefully sits, stares at a point just past your left ear, and laughs at odd moments. With house repairs, norovirus, Caroline's pulled back right before she had to fly to NYC, preparing for our cruise over Spring Break, the girls getting their customary colds before setting out on a cruise, our normal hectic lives, and (all the while) trying to keep my classes running on course to complete the material for the Common Exam in June, I just need to shut down for a bit. So I realized that my stint at Haversaw High has all been a dream. In reality, I'm asleep on my multimillion-dollar yacht somewhere in the Mediterranean Sea, whiling away the time, awaiting the start of the Festival de Cannes in May.

I've had fun with the little fantasy and have incorporated all of my friends. Our art teacher has been commissioned to do the stained glass for the main entertainment area. Although, I'm a little concerned. She picked up a young Spaniard named Julio to work as her assistant. I can't see that he can do too much glasswork with his shirt off all the time. Sandy is a movie star sailing with us for the release of her newest film at the festival, and so forth. All of my co-workers have decided that, yes, I am crazy; but they like my delusions!

On a lighter note, my chemistry kids took a test on ionic compounds today. If you want a case study in the various ways facial expressions can convey emotions, then you should watch a group of students take a chemistry test. We had the perplexed shaking of the head, the focused stare upon the paper, the frantic flipping of pages hoping for inspiration, the dazed shock, and the triumphant smile of knowing the material. I now understand why my organic chemistry professor would laugh heartily at me while I took his tests. Apparently, I maintained the "What-the-%&*^%-was-I-thinking-when-I-signed-up-for-this-course" expression on my face whenever I took one of his tests.

They say a good teacher should address the multiple learning styles of their students. Because I have a piece of paper that says I'm a master teacher, I instinctively know this fact. To address my students who learn best by physically manipulating objects, I added a tactile lesson (for those of you not in the know of educational jargon, tactile means touching things) where my students would use molecular models to create replicas of covalent compounds to determine their VSEPR shape. (VSEPR = Valence Shell Electron Pair Repulsion Theory...try to say that three times real fast.) While they were taking their test and providing free entertainment with their facial expressions of terror, I was gleefully envisioning how well they would understand why H_2, O_2, and N_2 would form a linear shape based on their bonding patterns. I imagined the activity stimulating higher-order thinking skills as the students worked out the structural formula for C_2H_5Cl and how this would be the spark that inspired one of my students to chemistry greatness, even citing me as their inspiration when he or she accepted the Nobel Prize in this noble field of science. Instead, my students used the multitude of spheres and sticks (think Tinker-toys) to create dogs, bobble heads, and hats. One kid even made an ingenious mask, which bore exactly no resemblance to the animal face he claimed it represented. Yes, the experts really know what the *^#@ they are talking about!

3-15-2013
Friday

I will forgo any references to thanking God for Friday, but the Lord only knows we're whipped. One of my friends just walked in saying in his twenty-plus years of teaching, he has never needed a vacation more than this year. I agree. That's why we're forking over the money for a cruise so that we can leave our worries and cares behind. Because it's a Disney Cruise, I doubt if we're going to get stranded somewhere in the Gulf of Mexico with no toilets. It's been a rough year for both the Carnival Cruise Line and me. I've chronicled my issues with my first semester previously in this narrative, but it is important to stress that you can have too many kids in a class. Yes, in college you can have hundreds of students in a lecture hall, but you must remember, these are highly motivated adults who are paying a butt-load of money to sit in that lecture hall. Not kids, who to say it nicely, could give a rat's ass about education. Even so, I do not mind teaching these kids. But, you can't shove 34 kids who would rather be anywhere else in the world than sitting in my classroom and expect me, the teacher, to be able to work miracles. It won't happen. In reality, the *Bad News Bears* get eliminated in the first game of the playoffs. The socially awkward kid doesn't get the prom queen in the end. Those are Hollywood tales. We believe in them because they give us hope, because deep down we always pull for the underdog. Unfortunately, in the real world, the underdog is beaten far more than he wins. That, in a nutshell, is education. Teachers pull for those underdog kids, even though most will not make it past high school. We go into that classroom, time and time again, hoping against hope, that one of those underdogs will make it this time. Overcrowding makes that prospect next to impossible. There just isn't enough of me to help all of those kids.

At Haversaw, we're on a bizarre hybrid schedule where some classes meet every day for a semester while others meet every other day for the entire year. Both types of classes last for 90 minutes each. That's a long time to sit in one class, and both my wife, and my previously mentioned friend who is in dire need of a vacation, can stress that the alternating days schedule is a nightmare. This has added stress to our plates, so to speak.

The political situation for the past two years has been terrifying for teachers. I'm facing the very real possibility of losing all of my plans for retirement if the politicians carry out their intent of dismantling the pension plan that they agreed to provide twenty years ago. We've had more and more demands placed on us, and our pay has been stagnant for years.

Let me also take a moment to clear up some misconceptions. Teachers are not always clamoring for more money. Most of us did not get into this profession for the pay. But, I would like to be paid on the scale the law said I should be and not have the people making the laws change the scale each year. I have a friend who is in her fifth year of teaching and is still making what was a first-year teacher's salary because they keep changing the pay scale. You do not want to see what a first year teacher's pay is now. There's a very good reason why we can't fill teaching positions while unemployment remains chronically high in North Carolina. This is what angers teachers as it should enrage anyone who's been put through it. When you sign a contract that states you get X amount of a pay increase each year, you should bloody well get that increase or do away with the damn scale.

On a final note, we were sent a survey by someone in Capital City gauging teacher frustration. It focused upon the new evaluation tool and the merit-based pay. I think I've already mentioned how much merit-based pay, that is already state law, I've received in the past five years. If I haven't, it's zero. So, if they implement merit-based pay, my question is will they live up to their commitments or simply change the law so they don't have to honor their own agreement?

It's been a stressful year. Like my friend, I'm in desperate need of a vacation.

3-18-2013
Monday

It's the time of the year when students who couldn't care less about mathematics of any source become masters in the field of statistics. Technically, gambling is illegal in NC schools, but during March Madness, brackets are everywhere and topics turn to discussions concerning win/loss records, net efficiency, and strength of schedule. All, of course, in a purely academic sense; think of it as an application in probability.

It's also a time of madness of a different source. During the month of March, our Parenting class issues the dreaded robotic babies to their soon-to-be teenage parents. After a pregnancy lasting, at most, twenty minutes, the students become proud parents of an entirely life-like baby doll that does everything except projectile vomit. These dolls cry, demand attention, and even have motion/pressure sensors that penalize rough handling by the parent. I found this out the hard way when, being completely unaware of the advances made in baby simulation technology, I knocked a doll off of the desk of one of my students as a joke. I had to beg the teacher to not fail the girl for the assignment.

This year I had a tale of two girls in my fourth period. Sally couldn't wait to get her doll and talked longingly of having babies once she was old enough. Brittany, on the other hand, dreaded the very thought of having a child. Last year she killed her "baby" three or four times. Her experience with the baby simulation was nothing short of horrible. It started with being verbally attacked in Wal-Mart by a self-righteous woman who was eager to condemn Brittany for the abomination of having a child at such a young age. During the night the baby would not stop crying, so Brittany marshaled her maternal instincts and threw it in the closet. That morning, the sleep-deprived Brittany failed to protect her precious child from its grandmother, who proceeded to knock the head off of the poor simulator.

The best story she told was how she managed to cope with the difficulties of juggling motherhood and athletics. Unable to obtain proper childcare, Brittany proceeded to shove the poor baby into her field hockey pads. She dropped it once trying to stop a goal, and then held it roughly by the neck as she ran down the field. The police, who were called in to investigate the allegations of gross child abuse, found the situation highly humorous when both Brittany and her coach explained that it wasn't a real baby. Apparently an elderly neighbor was horrified at the sight of the baby being manhandled on the field.

7

The First Day of Spring

3-20-2013
Wednesday

It's the first day of spring, bringing with it a sense of renewal, rebirth, and the imminent approach of Spring Break. The day, while still holding the lingering bite of winter, was supposed to warm nicely to near 60 degrees. So I was in a good mood when I pulled into the parking lot of Haversaw High. A mood enhanced by observing our JROTC kids practicing a competition maneuver. Like a synchronized machine, they quickly strung a line between two stately oak trees, and had quickly shimmied across the intervening space. For the final step, they were required to remove the rope, which makes sense. If you are undergoing covert operations, the last thing you would want to do is leave up a honking big calling card in the form of a rope stretched across a river with a sign on it saying, "Please ignore this rope. We're not on your side of the river planning to blow something up, or anything of the sort."

To remedy this situation, one kid started the process of unraveling the rope from its anchor hold while another kid did the same for the other tree. Then all five men (I use this term as a mark of honor. Any kids entertaining the thought of protecting our country, as these boys have, deserve to be called men. I would also had added women, but the group was comprised entirely of men.) pulled in unison while a sixth person monitored the situation for any snags. Unfortunately, the sixth man forgot to unhook his harness from the rope and was quickly pulled to the ground. (Think of a 5 vs. 1 match of tug-of-war) It was hilarious. For the record, the kid was unharmed and laughed as well.

So, it was with high hopes that I entered Haversaw's SIT (School Improvement Team) meeting. This sounds like a lofty goal, and indeed in its purest sense it is a noble endeavor; however, the system, state, and federal government mandate most of what occurs in a school. The reality is that SIT can do little to improve the school, or anything else of the sort. Most of us view our term on SIT as a two-year stint in prison. Realistically, we can influence budget allocations, discipline policy for minor infractions (the major ones are controlled by the school system), and school beautification issues (although at Haversaw, a fellow teacher had to submit three plans and receive three different approvals from various central office personnel for her club to plant a tree); however, most meetings end in pointless squabbles over issues where we exercise little authority.

The meetings should be a means by which Mr. Flair shares information with the SIT representatives and we, in turn, share with our departments. But instead, human nature asserts itself and the bickering quickly commences. This particular meeting began in just such a manner, and my spiral from carefree and happy, to grumpy, caustic teacher began.

Our first item on the agenda sounded like a label that should be placed on a party invitation. The Haversaw system is moving toward the adoption of a BYOD policy. As I said, an acronym that conjures images of drunken revelers but actually means Bring Your Own Device. To phrase it a little differently, it's a policy that will allow students to use their smartphones, tablets, or laptops to access the school network. Current policy does not allow the use of such devices inside of a school building. This sounds like a good idea. There have been many times when it would have been easy to tell the kids to look up the information on their phones and, to be perfectly honest, I did just that and hoped Mr. Flair didn't come by the room for a pop-in observation. Another consideration for this policy is that the kids have this technology at their disposal, so why not let them use it to enhance their education instead of having their parents wasting their money on a data plan so their child can either download the latest grumpy cat video or become heavily involved in whatever Twitter war was currently being waged at that particular second. As long as our network is large enough to handle the increased load, then I'm all for this policy.

As with all things, the devil is in the details. First, our school system feels that we're too stupid to use this technology without the explicit guidance of the central office staff. So, in order to allow the students to use their mobile devices in my classroom, I would be required to undergo thirty-five hours of training. Now, on the surface, this sounds good. In theory, during the training I would learn how to integrate various different devices into a lesson and troubleshooting techniques when it all goes wrong. However, the training does not address the minor issue of technology. Instead, it focuses on pedagogy issues of developing lessons using technology. (For those of you not in the know, pedagogy is a fancy word that means teaching; it just makes people sound smarter.)

The nail in the coffin for my support came when the real issue was broached that not everyone has such a device. I know it is shocking, but not all parents are willing to shell out hundreds of dollars for a phone and the additional expense of a data plan. When I polled my class, I found that over half of the students either did not have a phone or were using a phone without a data plan. How do you deal with this situation? For me, I would let them pair up with someone who does have such a device. End of problem. But, we're a public school, and if one kid has access to something, all kids must have equal access. The school would have to provide a smart device for the kids without one. In essence, cash-strapped Haversaw High would be required to buy iPhones for kids without one.

My mood worsened. Next, we proceeded to gripe for about twenty minutes on issues over which we have no control. I hate having my time wasted, and boy did this discussion waste my time. For some strange reason, I do not think the sheriff's deputy controlling the traffic flow cares one bit that teacher X feels the deputy is funneling too many cars of parents wanting to pick up their children from the Haversaw Highway into the parking lot. Apparently, teacher X feels that it is more important that his car is blocked in the parking lot for fifteen minutes instead of clearing traffic off of a four-lane highway and preventing a seventy-car pile-up.

Finally, we started discussing an issue that SIT could mandate—the dress code. All in all, our students do not violate the dress code at Haversaw High. Yes, a few guys wear saggy britches, and sometimes a girl may—gasp!—show a bare shoulder with a bra strap or show some cleavage, but the dress code is not a real issue, by and large. The saggy britches are usually accompanied by a clean pair of boxers, and rarely do I have to worry about the stress-breaking point of a particular type of fabric stretched to its maximum capacity over the chest of a buxom student. Although we did have one student show up in a t-shirt with a huge smiley face on the front. In tiny print at the bottom was the caption, "Boobies Make Me Smile." Whether humorous or offensive, the boy was sent home. Jennifer, the teacher who reported it, thought it was hysterical.

So, dress code is not a major issue at Haversaw High. However, a group of teachers are waging a personal war against leggings. If you are not aware of this fashion trend, leggings are tighter than pants, but don't look like tights. Mckenzie and Kaitlyn wear them all the time. For some reason, this style has been deemed offensive, distracting, and basically shakes the moral foundation of our society. For my part, I don't even notice it when my female students wear them. And, aside from a comment I heard in the hallway when one boy told another boy that he loved spandex after they had followed two young ladies down the hall, I rarely hear the issue discussed. Before you accuse me of condoning chauvinistic behavior, the girls overheard the comment and giggled furiously. Nobody was offended, so it was not a problem.

In our meeting, it was suggested that all the teachers inspect their students for dress code violations such as low-cut necklines, sagging pants, or the offensive leggings that most people don't notice. Once again, at face value, this seems like a great idea. But let's consider it from my perspective. I'm a forty-two-year-old man. My orders are to visual inspect the amount of cleavage shown by female students and to study their butts to see if they are, indeed, wearing leggings and not just tight jeans. While I am trying to ascertain if the female student, who more than likely is underage, is in compliance with Haversaw's dress code, Johnny films it on his iPhone the school system bought for him. Within minutes, a video of my inspection is posted on Facebook, Instagram, Snapchat, and YouTube with the tagline of "Teacher Staring at Girls' Butts." I send Suzy out of the room, thus incurring her wrath for challenging her right to wear a ninety-dollar pair of leggings her mother thought were cute. Before she makes it to the office, the underage girl has now tweeted how I was staring at her butt. Suzy's mom reads the tweet, checks out the video, forwards all of this to the local paper, and before lunch I'm on administrative leave without pay with probable jail time to follow. Am I paranoid? Hell yes! On top of all of this, a bill was just introduced on the Senate floor in Capital City where Senator Toole wants to remove my right to due process, aka tenure, so I can be fired at a whim for such things as providing bad publicity in the local paper…like ogling the butts of my students.

3-22-2013
Friday

I had to miss school yesterday. There's not much you can do when your younger child wakes up with a 102 degree fever. Fortunately, it was a case of the wrong antibiotic she had received on Monday for a sinus infection. After a dose of the new antibiotics, she's up and running today. Yesterday, all she wanted to do was snuggle with me on the couch. This had two benefits. One, I know that these days when mom and dad are the greatest people on the face of the planet are fast coming to an end. While I would rather she not be sick, I'll enjoy it when she wants to cuddle with her dear old dad. Second, it was the first real day of March Madness. All day on a couch with my little girl asleep in my arms and basketball on the TV, well, it doesn't get much better than that.

On a more serious note, I was reminded of a Pink Floyd song from the album *The Wall.* During our faculty meeting today many teachers were complaining about the fourteen-day exam schedule for eight exams. With mandated on-line testing, Common Exams, and the inherent problems with their scoring, and ridiculously long state-mandated End of Course exams, we just can't get everything done in less time. That's more instructional time taken from my classes. I have received orders from Capital City demanding excellent scores or else they will fire my butt once they remove the protection of due process for job termination from teachers. It has ceased to faze me anymore. In essence, I'm comfortably numb.

3-27-2013
Wednesday

SPRING BREAK!!!

4-8-2013
Monday

Reality bites. This simple phrase gleaned from the 1994 movie titled *Reality Bites* can become evident in various circumstances.

It may be when a spouse sues for divorce or when your cherished pet dies. For me, it hit this morning when I made a pot of coffee for Caroline. For eight days we were treated like royalty during our cruise. Our every whim was granted (sometimes for a price, but it was granted nonetheless) with gracious ease. The finest coffees were offered, teas from around the world were imbibed, and Mckenzie and Kaitlyn drank enough Diet Coke to clog their bladders. We sampled gourmet delights beyond description. The Chicken Parmesan was so scrumptious my life is now complete. From a culinary point of view, I have nothing left to live for. I will never taste anything as fine as that morsel.

Between the food, the games, the ports-of-call, the relaxation, and the simple time together as a family, the cruise was a time of recuperation. It has been a stressful year and I'm afraid the years are only going to get worse until I retire. That is, of course, if they leave me a pension so I can retire. Both Caroline and I needed some time to immerse ourselves in a fantasy world where our cares were left upon the shore.

This morning, the simple act of having to make my own pot of coffee brought that fantasy to a screeching halt and reality hit with the force of the proverbial ton of bricks. As I said, reality bites.

The school day, though, was enjoyable, if such a word is applicable to going back to work on the day after you return from a Disney Cruise. It was fun to listen to the kids talk about their adventures and trips. Even the kids who worked the entire break said they enjoyed not having to squeeze in time for homework. Although one guy who complained about the snow and sleet last Thursday about threw his chemistry book at me when I informed him it was eighty-five degrees in Key West on that particular day. All of the students got a laugh at my expense when I turned green and stared at them in an odd manner.

"What's wrong, Mr. Gregory?" Susie asked.

"You're all swaying back and forth," I answered.

After eight days at sea, my equilibrium has yet to return to normal. At odd moments, the world would suddenly lurch and sway as if I were still on the ship. After a few moments of confusion, one guy yelled, "Hey, Mr. Gregory's landsick."

4-12-2013
Friday

I don't know which is longer, an eternity in Hell or the week back to work after a great vacation. Needless to say, we're all ready for the weekend, especially when we started the day off like today with the announcement that the storms of last night knocked out our Internet. When I first started teaching, this announcement would have been met with amused laughter. Most rooms lacked a computer. Today it invoked panicked looks of terror. Teachers were scrambling to find something to fill the void in their classrooms now that their large monitors (which look suspiciously like flat screen HD TVs, but don't tell the central office), Internet-based educational software, and network-shared PowerPoint presentations were rendered useless by the simple fact that the network crashed with the Internet. For years, my coworkers have ridiculed me for my old-school teaching methods. (Okay, that's a little harsh imagery. Actually they just make fun of me for using too many whiteboard markers.) But now, the time to laugh was mine. To date I have never had my trusty board and marker crash from a storm. Now if I could just print off a blasted class roster, I would be set. Classroom attendance is done via the computer network and the Internet.

On a more serious note, I just finished grading a set of chemistry tests dealing with the topics of compound molar mass, percent composition, and empirical formulas. All worthwhile topics, I am sure, which will be desperately needed in the life of the non-chemist. This semester I have all honors chemistry classes, so they need to be challenged. According to the grades of one class, this test definitely succeeded in that department.

After twenty years of teaching, I have not been able to explain why some kids "get it" and other kids don't. This is the heart of the debate concerning the failings of schools across America. The argument goes along the lines that all kids can learn; therefore, if they fail, it is not the fault of the student, it must be the fault of the teacher. If the teacher inspired the students to learn by using (insert name of latest educational fad here) approach, all students would achieve greatness. Some say that we should push the use of technology to encourage students to become actively engaged in the learning process. In the case of technology, I have observed that the only active learning is the students trying to actively bypass the firewalls so they can download dirty pictures or play video games. Now, I will admit that I am both cynical about any new reforms and am a self-professed "old school" teacher, but I'm not an idiot. I observe and I listen, and I also have access to hundreds of students who are being taught with whatever fad is currently in vogue. I am also a damn good teacher. So when I say something doesn't work nearly as well as the media and politicians claim, I am not simply crying, "Wolf!"

In my classes, I have found that some kids are able to process information better than others. To me, this makes sense. Not everyone can throw a 95-mph fastball or consistently hit 3-point jump shots. In sports, it's understood that not everyone is equal. You have your elite, and they move on to achieve fame and fortune playing professional sports. While practice will hone the skills you have, it is very rare to find a short person in the NBA. However, in education it is expected that all the students are little robots and that by inserting input using a prescribed method, they will all fully grasp the functions they are to accomplish. If this doesn't happen, than either the teacher is incompetent or the student is not trying. I'm here to tell you that both are a load of (insert whatever vile, stinky, concoction you can imagine here). I have taught my heart out using multiple styles of teaching more times than I care to remember, only to have my classes perform poorly on a test. Likewise, I have seen students try until it brings tears to your eyes, only to see them fail time and time again. Who is at fault?

4-15-2013

Monday

Oh, God. I have friends and fellow teachers who qualified to run in the Boston Marathon. Thankfully, they are all safe.

4-16-2013

Tuesday

After the NCAA tournament is finished and the nets have been cut down, the basketball world's attention becomes focused upon who is staying in college basketball and who is throwing their lots in with the NBA. Can (insert name of a championship coach) pull together enough recruits to replace those that are leaving? Something similar happens in the Haversaw System as well. It's called the transfer fair.

At the beginning of April, the announcement is made that our declaration-of-intent forms are due. This form lets a principal know who is retiring, who is leaving the system altogether, and who desires to transfer to a new school. Once declarations have been made, then the fun begins. First it's the whispered discussions in the hallways. "Did you hear Mary signed up for a transfer?" or "What have you heard about Jefferson High School?" Teachers, like the rest of humanity, enjoy a little bit of gossip now and then, so this is to be expected. The teachers who apply for a transfer tend to keep it quiet, but somehow word always leaks.

Some parents have asked over the years why a teacher would want to leave an established position and reach the obvious con-

124

clusion that something must be wrong with that teacher's performance. Teachers are human and sometimes make mistakes, and the easiest way to correct that mistake is to start over. But this is only part of the answer, and realistically only a small percentage of teachers transfer to hide a less-than-stellar past.

Sometimes an excellent teacher will leave a school or school system because of a disagreement in policy. Over twelve years ago, I fled the block system that was to be implemented in my old school system. I hate the block system, and coupled with some interesting interpretations wherein the superintendent outright lied as to our reasons for switching to this system in a community meeting, and some strange policies of my principal, I quit and went to work at Haversaw High. I managed to keep from having to teach on the 90-minute block system for almost a decade before Haversaw Schools finally caved in to pressure from the state.

Sometimes teachers will transfer due to disagreements with coworkers. All of the drama and angst we experienced in middle school and high school did not vanish when we entered adulthood. It would be nice to think that the human race would outgrow pettiness and focus upon things that are truly important, but we don't. I've been involved in several feuds over the years, and I will probably be involved in several more before I retire. While we try to present a united front to the kids and continue to offer excellent educational services, it does make for a tough working environment. An environment that some feel is better to leave. Sometimes it's just easier to start over at a new school.

Finally, a teacher may leave because they simply want a change. At times, the walls of your classroom begin to loom, the idea of teaching the same course yet again gnaws at your will, and your professional life becomes stale. A change is needed, so a transfer is sought.

For reasons wholly her own, which I will not share here, Sally, my colleague and good friend for the past thirteen years, has sought and been granted a transfer. New life has been breathed into her, and she is happier than I've seen her for the past two years. She's already started the process of packing up her room, choosing what to keep and what to discard. Teachers are notorious packrats, and sometimes the only time we truly find out what we have is when we have to move to a new room, or in Sally's case, a room at a new school. As a professional, I'm happy for her. As a friend, I know this is best for her. But I feel like I've been kicked in the solar plexus every time I enter her room and see a new box. I've said goodbye to a lot of people over the years. Some have moved to new towns, some have transferred to new schools, and some have left the profession altogether. It sucked seventeen years ago when I first said goodbye to Kim when she left to start a career in administration, it sucked when Ashley left seven years ago to return to her hometown, it sucked when Mark followed his wife to a new town four years ago, and it sucks now. I hate goodbyes.

4-18-2013

Thursday

A wise principal once told Caroline that he started every morning by reading the paper to see if his school was in the news for that day. If you still live in the fantasy world where the press actually supported the efforts of schools and would publicize pleasant news stories about education, then I envy you. For me that thought was dashed upon the hard rocks of reality years ago. The teachers can work their butts off to teach, encourage, nurture, etc. the kids under their care, and, if a supportive story is printed, it is usually buried in the depths of the paper. Every now and then, I will read a "feel-good" story printed on the front page of the local section; but, as a general rule, if the story doesn't include athletics, it's not printed. Now, let there be a fight on campus or improper conduct of a teacher, whether substantiated or not, and then it's front-page news. So whenever a news story concerning education appears in print, it is usually not a good thing.

Today, buried in the front section of the Haversaw Daily, I found a summary of a bill introduced in the North Carolina General Assembly. The crux of the would-be law is to eliminate the cap size on lower elementary classes. First high school, then middle school class size limits were scrapped a few years ago when the economy tanked. That's why last semester I topped one hundred kids in only three class periods. This semester is better with fewer than ninety kids in my three sections. When I started teaching, this would have been impossible. At some point in the past (I believe it may have been after the Baby Boomers graduated) government leaders had the wisdom to realize that one teacher can only do so much. In my case, national safety standards state that it is unsafe to hold a laboratory exercise with more than twenty-five students in a classroom. In my earth sciences, I blew that figure out of the water, and my numbers aren't too good in my chemistry classes this semester. However, state and national science standards mandate laboratory activities in all science classes. So I hold my labs, try to idiot proof the directions, and pray nobody gets hurt. Because I can assure you, if somebody gets hurt, it will not be the state leaders who are held as negligent, it will be me.

Now they want to increase the size of kindergarten and first grade classes while they are eliminating teachers' aides. The law is phrased in a manner that implies the legislation is not eliminating positions, rather it is providing "flexibility" for school systems to distribute state monies as they see fit. The reality, however, is that if more budget cuts are forced on the schools, which it looks like is going to happen, and there is not the protection of a classroom cap on the number of students, then you can be assured that the classroom sizes will increase. I had a hard enough time getting my two kids to the bathroom when they were that age, I can't imagine what it will be like to herd thirty five-year olds to the bathroom, much less try to teach them.

On a lighter note, I visited a fellow teacher whom we will name Bob. As I walked by his room, Bob motioned for me to enter.

"Hey, Mr. Gregory," he said. "You know my final evaluation for the year is approaching, don't you."

"Yes," I replied. "Mine's today."

Bob said, "I'm worried about Standard II Subsection 2a (we have a fourteen page evaluation form, if you did not know) that states Teachers provide an environment in which each child has a positive, nurturing relationship with caring adults. Teachers encourage an environment that is inviting, respectful, supportive, inclusive, and flexible. So, I'm practicing being nurturing with my students."

One girl looked up at me with pleading eyes and said, "Please make him stop. He hasn't insulted us once today, and he's saying things like 'Neato' and 'Swell.' Mr. Gregory, he's frightening us. We want the old Bob back."

I just laughed. People don't understand that teachers have different personalities. While you have a few bad apples who are verbally abusive to their students, there are rules and regulations in place to remove them from the classroom. If you hear insults, caustic comments, or just plain bad jokes, the kids know we're not serious. Neither Bob or I would never dream of picking on a shy kid. We trade friendly barbs with the class clowns, the confident students, and even the ones who just need a little bit of attention. When well-meaning professionals try to mandate teacher behavior, they force us into roles that are alien to us. To be honest, it is a little frightening to watch and the kids know if you're not sincere. They also know Bob would stand up for any of them and they love him for it.

A Question:

I wish someone could explain this to me. If I were to hack into a student's social media account such as Facebook or Twitter, and spread all of the personal information they had listed around to the rest of the school, I would justifiably be branded a bastard and would face professional censure and possibly criminal charges. All of these punishments are more than justified in this situation. If a student, however, hacks into a teacher's account and spreads his/her personal information to the school, it's viewed as a joke. This happened to a friend of mine today, and for some reason, I don't think this is too fair.

4-19-2013
Friday

I started today with a professional learning community (PLC) meeting. While I enjoy interacting with my colleagues, the forced conditions of a PLC bring to mind all of the thousands of things needing to be done—not the least of which is the fact that my room is trashed from various labs and is in serious need of cleaning—to the forefront of my consciousness. Needless to say, PLCs tend to make me grouchy. This one had the double affront of me having to tell kids they could not make up missed tests because of the PLC, and once the meeting started, we discussed the latest legislature movement to cut my pay. Even though it is standard practice in industry, which these legislators think education should mimic, to pay employees with the highest credentials higher pay, these people want to cut the pay of teachers with master's degrees and national certification. Caroline and I have both, so this will be a double whammy in my house. Somehow, the Old North State is going to cut the pay of the highest qualified teachers, cut funding to the schools by millions, allow the overall pay of teachers to stagnate to where we are ranked somewhere in the realms of Satan's dominion in comparison to other states, and increase class size to where I will have taught over 180 students in just six classes, and still lead the nation in academic excellence by recruiting to nation's top teaching talent. I'm having a hard time seeing it.

All of this took a backseat in the level of importance though as kids came into my class later that morning glued to their cellphones following the progress of the manhunt in Boston. Questions about mole ratios and converting molar masses of reactants to grams in stoichiometry problems were intermingled with exploring the motives of two young immigrants to America that would lead them to enact acts of terrorism. My problems faded into the background amidst scenes of Americans, liberal and conservative, coming together in prayer and unity for a city inflicted with a horrific crime. I just wish it would not take a tragedy to remind us that we're all Americans, that we are all "one nation under God with liberty and justice for all."

4-22-2013
Monday

The day has started bright and sunny, which is a far cry from the way Friday ended. A strong cold front moved across the area, wreaking havoc across the nation. At 3:42 pm, exactly two minutes after we dismissed school, the call came from the central office stating that Haversaw County was under a tornado warning. Emergency protocol went into effect. Buses on the road were redirected to the nearest school, buses on the lot were unloaded and the kids were sent to a safe location, any kids not in their parent's car, were hurriedly ushered into a building for the duration of the warning. Outside of one kid acting like a fool, the students on campus proceeded in an orderly manner once we were able to convey that this was real and not a drill. I was proud of them.

The parents, for the most part understood that school board policy, if not state law, forbade Haversaw High from releasing any students from the school in the face of potential danger. When the wind's intensity increased, a lot of the parents opted for the safety of the main building instead of the comfort of their cars. One older brother, who was trying to pick-up his sister, was not so understanding. After issuing a string of obscenities at the secretaries, he was escorted out of the building by our sheriff's deputy. I understand it was an inconvenience, and I'm sure the young man had places to go, but sometimes the need to provide a safe environment for the kids overrides the consideration of the caregivers. My own child was on a bus somewhere and I would much rather have preferred seeing to Kaitlyn's safety than listening to an irate older brother who didn't understand why we wouldn't let him take his sister from the safety of brick building into a potential tornado. It turns out Kaitlyn was safe at a local elementary school, so no harm was done.

I don't know if it is the bright day, the cooler weather, or the fact that we're not facing an eminent natural disaster, but I'm in a good mood today. There is a spring to my step today, and I feel like I can actually teach stoichiometry, thermochemistry, solutions, and acids and bases by the end of May. Possibly, they won't need a shovel to find my test scores after all.

4-24-2013

Wednesday

Apparently I have single-handedly destroyed three students' life-long dream to become doctors. After slamming a pencil onto a table, one of the three asked me if she would need to know limiting reactant problems to get into med-school. While I answered I was not certain about med-school, I did know most doctors begin as chemists or biologists, and that, yes, she would need to know how to do stoichiometry and the rest of chemistry for those majors.

"I don't see what chemistry has to do with being a doctor," she said. Her whine was followed by her two fellow dreamers.

"Well," I replied. "It is a good idea for a doctor to have a working knowledge of chemistry, so she will know what the medications are doing inside of her patients' bodies."

131

The young girl looked at me with a quizzical expression on her face and said, "I don't understand what chemistry has to do with drugs."

At that point, there really wasn't much I could say in response.

4-26-2013

Friday

Can I flag down the bus driver for the planet Earth and get him to stop? I want to get off now.

The day started by reading about yet more asinine antics of our school board in the paper. Apparently, Haversaw Schools were just awarded nearly $20 million in grant money from the federal government, and our school board is upset about it. Not the $20 million mind you, but the $500,000 that was appropriated for the enrollment of the principals of low performing schools into a particular training program. It seems that one of the co-authors of the program, which has been proven to be effective, was reported to be Muslim, Buddhist, and possibly a pacifist terrorist. Okay, I made that up, but the real reasons for the lack of support for this program were equally ludicrous. One school board member went so far as to call the federal grant money "Funny Money" and that he resented the way the grant mandated the uses of the money.

What's funny to me is the fact that all of this was spelled out in detail when these same school board members applied for the grant. Entities, be they private or public, do not simply hand out $20 million for you to use at your discretion. Grants, by their nature, spell out exactly how the money is to be used. I know. I've applied for several of them. Every detail is specified. So, I'm surprised that Johnny, the school board member, either didn't read the original grant in which he was more than happy to accept, or this particular program has become politically charged. From what I've read about it, the program has the audacity to promote critical thinking of the participants, and—gasp—the idea that maybe we can all get along. Yep, this sounds like a communist plot to destabilize our government if ever I've seen one.

Another possibility for the misunderstanding is that our elected official, Johnny school board member, lacks a basic understanding of how a grant actually works. I'm not certain which is scarier. The same school board member went on to distinguish himself in this article by saying, "We wouldn't spend this kind of money if it was our own money."

I may be out of line in saying this but if some rich relative were to offer to pay for my flight, lodgings, and tickets to the NBA finals, I would have no qualm in accepting his offer. Would I spend this kind of money if it were coming out of my budget? No, there's no possible way I could afford it. But if Uncle Moneybags wants to pay for it, I'll go and have a great time. That's why you apply for grants. You use the money to pay for things, like beneficial job training, that you would not normally have the money to do. If you don't like the program, then you should never have accepted the grant in the first place.

Already in foul mood, I received an urgent text from Caroline. It is never a good thing when you read a text stating, "CALL NOW!" In this case, she had been docked two days-worth of pay for having surgery. I'm sure it was a clerical mistake, but that's almost $600 we thought was safely in our bank account. Thankfully, we still have some of the inheritance money from my grandmother to tide us over until we get this sorted out, but this is ridiculous.

With Caroline calmed down to the point she was not going to hire a lawyer and march to the central office with pitchfork and lighted torch held high, I returned to my faculty meeting. Mr. Flair was standing in front of the auditorium, commenting that we would not be able to read the PowerPoint on display. My first comment, which thankfully I failed to utter, was "Well, with you standing in front of the projector, no, I can't."

The PowerPoint explained, in the exquisite detail used by people who love PowerPoint, how we were to open our EVAAS data. (Education Value-Added Assessment System) This is the program that tracks student performance from year to year. I am judged by how well my students improve from previous scores. Unfortunately, there has not been a previous science test, so I'm judged on how well my students performed on a reading test in eighth grade. I still haven't figured out how that judges my effectiveness as a science teacher. Our task, which is to be completed by May 12th, is to read the rosters of the students the EVAAS program says I have in my classes and verify that the roster is, indeed, correct. It turns out that some other school systems across the state are shifting students to protect the scores of favored teachers.

The final issue up for debate was how to handle early dismissals for prom. Due to the size of our student body, there are a limited number of venues that can house that rite of passage for our juniors and seniors. Even though I caution my students about the reality of the prom—that, while fun to dress up—the world doesn't change on prom night just because you chose to spend lavish sums of money on that day. In this case, the day will be on Friday, May 17th. The place we desired for the prom was booked solid for weddings every Saturday for the next two years. So, we're having prom on a school night. The last time we did this, the school was a veritable ghost town by the end of the day; every upperclassman in the school had signed out. Those who do not study history are doomed to repeat it. Well, we're repeating it. We'll see how it goes.

On a lighter note, my students took their stoichiometry test today. One student asked, "Mr. Gregory, is it possible to have a percent yield greater than 100%?" My answer will probably garner some complaints, but sometimes my mouth kicks in before my brain does. I replied, "Only if you're God."

8

"What have you done to screw up now?"

5-1-2013
Wednesday

"What have you done to screw up now, William?" was the question my mom asked me last night.

My answer was, "As far as I know, nothing, other than letting a kid charge his cell phone during class."

Events, which occurred Monday, prompted my mother's loving comments of support for my professional life. Between third and fourth periods, one of my former students approached me in the hallway and asked if he could charge his phone in my classroom. After a few moments of trepidation concerning the fact that I did not want to be responsible for a phone, I relented and took the foul device and its charger. Little did I know, he had already had an argument with his fourth period teacher over this very issue. Forty minutes later, I'm on the phone with one of our assistant principals being lectured on how teachers must present a unified front concerning the enforcement of school board policy.

I don't mind being taken to task when I've screwed up—although in this instance I do not think that letting a kid charge his phone in a classroom other than the one he is attending violates the policy stating students cannot use their cell phones during class. Apparently Verizon is now selling psychic implants that connect you to your phone telepathically.

However, I do take offense at the "butt chewing" occurring over the classroom phone while I am supposed to be teaching my students the intricacies of how the kinetic theory of matter explains the phases of matter. My assistant principal's parting words were to inform me that I now had permanent bus duty. This assignment is what prompted my mother's question as to my behavior as a teacher.

It turns out, that my misinterpretation of the cell phone policy had nothing to do with my new position as master of transportation distribution center. I've found that a fancy title helps ease the pain. John, the current transportation distribution master, is taking medical leave for prostate cancer, so they needed a male to help with crowd control. I fit the qualifications. I just can't wait until my raise kicks in. With a title containing the words "master" and "distribution," I'm betting my pay should jump to six figures. Yeah right. I get to stay at school twenty minutes later yelling at kids to quit making-out as they are waiting for a late bus, all for no extra pay or compensation.

My classes have reached a level of comfort such that my students find no fault in simply starting up a conversation about any topic regardless of the fact that I am furiously trying to cover four weeks worth of material in just three weeks. In fact, yesterday, I had my most spirited classroom discussion of the year. Unfortunately, it concerned a rumor that the UN was going to confiscate all weapons in the US and use them against us. I was able to offer succor for my student's fear as I explained to him that the UN lacks jurisdiction to take anything from US citizens and that this idea was used in a fictional account of the rapture by authors Tim LaHaye and Jerry Jenkins in the Left Behind series. So much for learning about the gas laws.

On a final note, today is my and Caroline's twentieth wedding anniversary. It doesn't seem like twenty years have passed, but when I looked at our prom picture she posted on Facebook, it looks like it. Caught up in a depth of emotions, I proceeded to state my feelings in a bit of romantic prose the likes of which would have made the great writers of history cry tears of joy for the simple pleasure of hearing these words strung together. When I had finished, flush with the knowledge that the fullness of my love had finally been expressed, Caroline, looked up from her iPad where she had been monitoring the comments posted in response to our picture, and said, "I'm sorry. Did you just say something?" I laughed until I cried. I love you, Caroline.

5-2-2013
Thursday

Today was already hectic before first period began. One of my students, I will refer to her as Betty, came in for her third attempt at finishing the stoichiometry test. Betty is a girl with severe ADHD, and chemistry has been nothing short of hell for her. It is a subject that requires intense concentration to complete multistep problems. As luck would have it, she is in fourth period, which is traditionally the worst class for students suffering from ADHD. The struggle of holding things together all day finally fails by the last period of the day. Neither she, nor her parents want her drugged, a decision with which I heartily agree. As long as the student does not use their impairment as an excuse to be a total jackass in class, I don't mind if attention wanders or if the seat seems to be filled with ants. To be truthful, I think I'm beginning to suffer from adult onset ADD, if such a beast exists. Of course, I could simply be losing my mind, but that's another story.

Needless to say, it has taken Betty a while to take this test. I don't mind. She's trying hard. However, today I'm covering an art teacher's class while he attends his daughter's kindergarten screening session. I had to frantically scramble to get my things arranged so I could cover the class while helping Betty with her test, and then three other kids came by to make up tests they missed for various field trips.

The irony of me becoming an art teacher, even if it's only for a class period, is that I couldn't draw my way out of a paper bag if my life depended on it and the bag was sopping wet. But, the kids were well behaved, and we teachers try to look out for one another. With the lack of support from Capital City, a superintendent who makes us take hourly sick leave for doctor's appointments even though we're salaried employees, and parent's screaming down our necks, if teachers didn't support each other, it sometimes feels like we wouldn't get any support at all.

Fortunately for Bart's class, he returned before I could give the class any pointers from my vast knowledge of artistic skills. You can only do so much with stick figures. I left Bart's room and settled into my thirty-year old chair located in our palatial workroom. A little bit of explanation may be in order at this point. The workroom consists of a space that was originally intended as a storage room, so it was, until recently, lined with large shelves. Last week, workers removed one row of shelves. It turns out the technology department needed some shelves to store excess equipment, so ours were taken. We're not upset, because it freed up some additional room for us.

The workroom is decorated in what can be only described as an industrial pipe motif. Steam pipes from some unknown heating source adorn one corner. We have no idea where the boiler is or where the steam goes because, as far as I know, no building or hallway at Haversaw uses radiators. I figure the steam is piped in directly from Hell, but I could be wrong.

The final bit of decoration is the eight-year old computer the technology department graciously allows us to use. Due to a programming glitch, it will only allow access to the state grading database, known as NCWise, for a select few people. I am not one of those select few. Our tech people have described the glitch to me, but I feel like my students when I explain molar mass to them. Because another teacher uses my room during my planning period, and I cannot log onto NCWise using the workroom computer, I am forced to use my teeny, tiny IBM notebook the teachers were assigned earlier in the year. Due to a combination of aging eyes and tiny screen, trying to actually see the spreadsheet to enter in the student grades is a feat in and of itself.

At the point where the headache caused by my squinting to see the screen was starting to develop, I heard the melodious chirp indicating an incoming message. Thankfully, I managed to stop myself from hitting the send button of the reply I had hastily typed in response to that message. It was from a parent blasting me for not updating my grades.

5-3-2013
Friday

The importance of sunlight cannot be underestimated. At 6:30 am, the sun poked its head out from behind the clouds for the first time in five days. A stationary front had taken up residency in Haversaw County for the past week. The overcast skies had created a cool, depressing malaise at Haversaw High. But today, the skies shone forth in blue glory illuminated by the wonders of the nuclear furnace found in the center of the Solar System. It's been a somber week. Some teachers like weeks such as this because it takes the edge off of students who are already picturing themselves having fun in the sun, but I don't like day after day of overcast skies. After a while, the subdued classes start to become monotonous and the days begin to drag. I needed the feel of the sunlight on my face, and today it made its grand reappearance. All was well, at least until my PLC started.

I won't bore you with the tedious discussions we had concerning the wording of a responsibility form intended to hold seniors accountable for their graduation by completing a teacher's class. At some point in the last twenty years, graduation became a right, not something you earned by hard work, responsibility, and perseverance. Now parents and political leaders view graduation to be a reward for attending a school, and attendance is optional. Furthermore, in my evaluation booklet (after the first few pages,

I ceased to call it a form) I am judged on how I, not the parents, ensure the graduation of all of my students.

With teachers receiving their orders to ensure all students will graduate, and schools judged on graduation rates, it is no surprise that graduation has become a farce across the state and nation. With our former principal, Mr. Peace, the students were very open with the fact that if you cried, he would let you walk across the stage and receive a diploma. So I'm just a tad bit dubious about any form holding students accountable for their graduation. Mr. Flair has not been tested yet to see if he will cave under the pressure, but I won't fault him if he does. I don't like it, but I understand that his job is as much on the line as is mine.

After the meeting, I decided to inquire about our future schedule. With the news that Sandy was transferring to a new school, Bob was tapped for the role of head scapegoat of the department. While the department chair does play a role in the hiring of new teachers and the assigning of teacher schedules, he also bears the brunt of the blame when things go wrong. I've been department chair once; I don't want to do it again. It's a lot of headaches for no extra pay. What amazes me is that some teachers will connive, lie, backstab peers, and more for the privilege of being department chair and the honor of carrying the Haversaw High torch to two extra meetings at the central office. Maybe I'm just immune to the sweet allure of power, but I just don't see why anyone would want it. Give me my bus duty any day over the chair.

Bob's answer to my question concerning my schedule was, "It's complicated."

This, of course, is not something you want to hear. "Complicated" means someone else is gunning to take over your classes, and the office is listening. In this case, it happens to be AP Environmental Science. Wendy, one of our current AP Environmental Science (aka APES) teachers, is retiring to pursue a career as an investment trader. By career, I mean she and her husband have acquired a considerable sum of money, and she is going to manage it. She's been taking classes concerning trading stocks and bonds for years and has done well with their "mock" account. She's talked for years about retiring, and I'm glad that she feels that the time is ripe for her to chase her dreams. Her announcement though freed up three APES classes. Bob teaches the other three and does not want the rest, preferring to keep his chemistry classes. Having a bit of insider trader status concerning Wendy's plans, I had made it known to Bob that I was interested in the course. At the time, nobody else was remotely interested in teaching APES.

Advanced Placement courses are viewed as the Holy Grail of classes in high school. It is believed that the kids are all great, you have no discipline issues, and all the kids will sit on the edge of their seats eagerly anticipating the next words of wisdom you are preparing to impart. The reality, as is usually the case, can be vastly different. For one, it is a college level course, so you wind up working your butt off preparing for it. Second, colleges are demanding their students take ever more numbers of AP courses, so the notion that only the best-of-the best sign up for the courses is false. Third, the parents are required to invest $80 per AP exam, with many students taking multiple courses, so the parents get justifiably angry if they feel their child is not prepared for the exam. I taught AP Biology before I moved to Haversaw, so I know from experience—the pressure placed on AP teachers is tremendous. However, I get bored when I teach the same thing for too many years in a row, and I have missed teaching the advanced material. Plus, I'm either a glutton for punishment, or slightly insane; only history will be able to tell for certain.

Enter Sara into the equation. Two months ago she was not interested in teaching another AP class. She had taught APES at another school and did not care for the experience. Now, with Wendy's announcement, Sara's tune has changed. Apparently, Mr. Flair is having trouble deciding who will teach what, so we're all in a state of limbo. AP courses require certification, so I need to know if I need to sign up for the required training. And with only one APES certification course being held in NC this summer, I really don't want it to fill up. We also have, at present, four positions that need hiring. Bob said we've filled two. That adds a whole new dimension to the equation. To sum it all up, it's a mess.

On a final note along the category of "People don't believe me when I tell them what happens at school," we had a student searched for the suspicion of bringing a weapon to school. It turns out she had a light saber in her backpack. Who knew Mr. Flair was a Sith Lord?

5-8-2013

Wednesday

There are times when I approach the end of the year at a sprint, ready to claim the accolades of the crowds for my stunning accomplishments; there are times when I approach the end of the year with eager anticipation for what adventures await as summer begins; and then there are the times, like now, where I feel like the marathon runner who collapses at the finish line. I was so tired today that I entered a hallway, made a left turn, and wondered who would have closed the door to the workroom. Thankfully, before I made a fool of myself, and quite possibly got arrested, some inner part of my brain finally sent the urgent message to my body that this was not the 900 Hallway, and the closed door was the entrance to the girls' restroom in the 200 Hallway.

On a different note, I have learned that I will be teaching at least two of the AP Environmental Sciences courses next year. In the exchange, I will lose my chemistry classes and complete the rest of my schedule with a combination of honors and regular earth and environmental sciences. All in all, not a bad schedule, although I must note with a hint of jealousy that other members in my department tend to have all honors classes, unless you count regular chemistry where the kids must be concurrently enrolled in algebra II, as a low-level course. The worst revelation to have

142

come out of our scheduling fiasco is that, once again, someone is trash-talking me in the office. As if this job isn't tough enough, now I have to deal with other teachers running to the office in an attempt to poison the administration against me.

Don't get me wrong, I'm not perfect, but I do try to give my best to whatever level of student I teach and I try to respect all of my students as human beings. However, in the guise of voicing "just a few concerns," these individuals are soon whispering rumor and wielding innuendo as if it were a blade to tarnish my image in the mind of whatever administrator will listen.

It's not just me, either. Every school has bottom feeders with aspirations of rising to the top, and their targets are varied. Some, justifiably, need to have concerns voiced about another teacher's behavior. In fact, state law mandates teachers to report any suspicions of inappropriate contact between teachers and students. However, most targets simply are in the way of the ghost whisperer's dreams of power. As if any teacher can truly have any real say in dictating policy. Most decisions are made at the system or state level, so these soul-suckers must content themselves with collecting the most desirable classroom and lording their schedule over the rest of us mere peons who have to dirty our hands with the flotsam and jetsam of the education world.

If it weren't directed at me, then I would think it was sad. Now I'm just pissed. I've been on the receiving end enough times, including being labeled a "burden to the department" during one school year when both of my daughters were hospitalized, and Mckenzie suffered from three additional bouts of pneumonia. My transgression, as far as I can ascertain, was to call a co-worker after a particularly hard night and ask her to find a video to show my class. It was a hard year, made worse by the accusations of, I'm hoping, well-intentioned coworkers. Thankfully, Sandy was the first person I ran into and she managed to calm me down to the level of only glaring at everyone I saw.

Today, Bob informed me that the meat-grinder of gossip was gearing up for another run. This information, coupled with the two rejection slips from literary agents I received this week, is making this week just peachy. I'm trying to focus upon the fact that we only have four weeks left.

On a happier note, Caroline's calculus kids felt very confident with their AP exam, and we received word that Jennifer, the teacher next door to me, had made a huge impact on a student's life. Sometimes, we need to hear that we are, indeed, making a difference.

5-9-2013
Thursday

It can't be good when one of your students says, "Mr. Gregory, I feel like my soul is crushed every time you open your [board] marker to begin the lesson." That's chemistry for you, although, for the record, I thought the lesson on making a dilute concentration was hardly worthy of destroying one's soul.

However, the day brightened at lunch when the office provided dessert for the staff. I think I traded my soul for a cookie.

5-10-2013
Friday

Have you ever tried to pee in absolute darkness? This was how I started my school day. After rushing to school, I decided to take a potty break before the faculty meeting started. As I entered the dark cavern of the Men's room, I hoped the automatic sensors would activate the lights. When the door shut, and the dark of midnight descended, I realized the sensors were either not activated or were busted. Thankfully, I had made it to the urinal before I became blind.

That was the highlight of the faculty meeting. As the meeting progressed from an exam schedule so complicated you needed a doctorate in quantum mechanics to understand it, into nit-picking about who exactly can sign out early for the prom, to the news that we were changing computer network systems yet again, I was left with the distinct thought that all of my righteous ire had been beaten out of me. The best I could do was utter a rebellious whimper. On the way out of the meeting, I told one teacher that I was done, and was just going to go run around in traffic. The teacher said she would join me, but only if we walked. That would limit the chances that a car might miss us.

On a more serious note, another teacher almost broke down into tears when she asked Mr. Flair to clarify how many disruptions we would have between now and our exams. Keep in mind, the stakes are so high on these exams that future raises and job evaluations depend on them. Mr. Flair rattled off "prom," "a state-wide exam for 10th graders," and "Awards Day." That's one major disruption each week until we give our exams, and that's not counting any field trips or play-off games that may pull individual students out of the classroom. I know kids need enrichment: and some of my fondest memories in high school come from extracurricular sources, but my teachers were not judged on their exam scores. The stakes are high, and I think we all sympathized with the young teacher. In this light, it did not surprise me to learn that one of the new science teachers hired to fill a position next school year has withdrawn her name for consideration. It turns out she would rather live in a developing nation working for the Peace Corp than teach in North Carolina.

T-minus seven days and counting for the prom. Forget about exams, forget about acids and bases, prom is the most important thing on students' minds now. Discussions range from where they are going to eat, to the status of the limo rental, what hairstyle are they going to have, and who is getting the alcohol for the after-prom parties. I'm pretty certain they didn't think I could hear the last one, but students fail to realize how far a whisper will carry. For me the excitement has dimmed over the years. After more than twenty proms, I've found that whether it is "One

Enchanted Evening," "A Night in the City," or even "The Titanic," they are all the same. Let's just say the luster of the fake jewels has become tarnished over time. This prom, I have the joy of guarding the punch. The excitement is just oozing out of every pore.*

    *For the record, while the prom has become a night I have to stay up well past my bedtime for the privilege of having sore feet and a head ringing from listening to loud music, I keep my grumpiness away from the kids. The prom was an important rite of passage when I was a teenager and it is an important rite of passage for my students. So I put on a smile and pretend I'm happy to be spending time away from my family.

5-15-2013
Wednesday

I had planned to write about the futility of useless debate concerning topics over which we have no control or influence. Today's entry was to have been about the frustration of fighting the tide of technology in the form of cell phones, which was the number one item from my morning meeting's agenda. Instead, perspective into what is truly important changed with a flurry of calls and text messages during my last SIT meeting. It began with a call from my mother-in-law, Deborah.

She's gotten a wee bit forgetful as she's aged and has issues with her cell phone, which is ironic considering the main focus of the SIT meeting, so it was not uncommon for Deborah to mistakenly dial my number instead of Caroline's. I dismissed the call and sent Caroline a text informing her that we were involved in a vital discussion concerning why I really didn't want to take up every kid's $600 iPhones and accept responsibility for it if it should go missing and that she needed to call her mother.

CALL IMMEDIATELY, was the response, a message that rarely acts as a prophesy for good tidings to follow. In this case, my father-in-law, Buck, had collapsed in the office of his eye doctor. Near blind and possessing a multitude of problems including partial deafness, he travels to Deacon Woods University Medical Center for his specialist physicians. If you're going to collapse with stroke-like symptoms, then you could pick a lot of worse sites in which to do it. Within minutes nurses and doctors surrounded Buck and Deborah, and he was quickly eased to the floor where doctors stabilized his systems. A gurney for the quick trip to the emergency room followed. With a quick word to Mrs. Purple informing her of my concerns that my father-in-law had just suffered a stroke, I headed to my room to prepare for my departure. Even though Mrs. Purple offered to pull plans together for me, that route is rarely good. Nobody benefits and this option should only be used in cases where it is impossible to create lesson plans. Thankfully, this was not a problem for me today. I don't know what possessed me to work my butt off Tuesday to finish the second part of my chemistry exam review and then not give it too the students, but I'm glad I did. It made leaving plans that much easier and I was quickly out of the door heading to Camelton, preparing for the worse.

Due to multiple foot surgeries last year, Caroline was left with no sick leave. We accrue a sick day each month. With a bad case of respiratory illness, norovirus, pulled back, and a funeral all in one year, Caroline had used all of hers and the administration can be less than helpful at times. At the end of the month, she will have earned a single sick day to carry into the next school year. Once I had determined that Buck was in stable condition, I advised Caroline to stay at school. While he had not suffered a stroke, the doctors were unsure as to what had caused the collapse. They wanted to run a battery of tests, and he would be admitted into the hospital. In what I knew was a futile gesture, I told my wife not to worry, I would handle everything.

I'm exhausted. Seven hours sitting in an ER will do that to you. I'm so tired I projected the notes on the monitor because I didn't trust myself to write them on the board. I spent the day babbling like an idiot. It's been a rough couple of days. But the grind of covering material continues. The State administrators don't care about sick relatives or days spent in the hospital. All homage is paid to the all important test scores. That's all that matters.

9

"Prom"

5-17-2013

Despite my prognostications of doom with the early dismissals and Friday prom, it went off without a hitch. I actually apologized to Mr. Flair for my doubts. He was pleased everyone behaved in a courteous and orderly manner.

The only real complaint I had was the fire drill and lock-down drill during fourth period. State law mandates we have these every so often and Mr. Flair decided to have it during the afternoon of the prom, figuring that so many junior and seniors had already left. The only problem was that I do not have an abundance of upperclassmen, and had planned to perform a titration lab, which takes the entire class period.

Prom was nice. No matter how much I complain, I like the prom. It's fun to see the kids dressed up, and even if I have to look the other way as they dance in a manner I know we never did when we were young (yeah right), I usually have a good time. It's sad watching some kids go all out for the prom. These are the kids who realistically will wind up working as tellers in grocery stores for their entire lives. For them this is truly one of the highlights of their lives. For others, the prom is merely one more rite-of-passage to experience on their journey to adulthood and a hoped for future of prosperity. Still, with the week we've had, I'm tired. By 10:00, the DJ announced, "Let's make some noise for the King and Queen!" My response to one of my coworkers was, "Let's make some noise because I am officially off the clock!"

(Happy Birthday!)
5-20-2013
Monday

Years ago, my birthday was not a time for joy, but a time for fear and trepidation. Apparently my mom had angered some Aztec or Mayan god of birthdays, and he forever cursed the day. If something bad happened, it happened on or near May 20th. I'm happy to report that the curse is still in effect. Caroline's dad is at home, but not because the doctors had found the cause for his collapse. Instead, they have run out of tests to perform that require hospitalization. In a nutshell, they don't know what the hell is going on with him. Blood pressure meds are affecting kidney function, sodium and magnesium levels are affecting heart rate, and so on. It's been an emotional roller coaster. So, at 11 o'clock last night, Caroline and I finally got her parents settled into their apartment. That would have been stressful enough for a weekend, but life doesn't take a vacation when your world is falling apartment.

Friday was the prom. This was one of the happiest moments in many a participant's life, so they didn't need a gloomy Mr. Gregory. Fortunately, I'm a bit of a thespian; once I entered the facilities, I donned my best "happy" face and pretended to enjoy myself. A friend's favorite quote concerning life is "Fake it until it's real." I faked it for all it was worth. I owed it to the kids.

Mckenzie's viola recital was Saturday night. She's worked hard, so between tag teaming at the hospital, Caroline and I worked to prepare Mckenzie for her big night. In the midst of all of this, I found out my mom was involved in enough family squabbles to last a lifetime. Roosters, utterly ignorant of things important, crow at dawn. Kids are like that as well. While old enough to be aware that something bad is happening with their grandfather, both Mckenzie and Kaitlyn continue with their lives with the ignorant bliss of children. So it was don the fake smile again and try to push the fears aside.

Both Caroline and I have played handbells for nearly all of our adult lives. It's a restful outlet for my musical talents. Plus, it's a good source for many a gag when I tell people I'm in a heavy metal band. Let me tell you, those low bells get pretty heavy at times. Our choir played both services yesterday and I was drafted to cover for a youth ringer whose soccer club was playing in the state semifinals. I was happy to do it, and I can now claim to have performed Coldplay's "Clocks" on hand bells. Kaitlyn also had her final choir performance last night. Caroline missed it because someone needed to be at the hospital. For a mother, this was devastating. I understand her pain. I missed a dance recital a few years back. It sucks.

I don't know how it is in other lines of work, but my job doesn't stop when family problems become overwhelming. The state testing deadlines are approaching with the speed of a bolt of lightning. Parents, while sympathetic, want the best for their child. They've already put up with two days of subpar teaching; tensions are mounting. Murmurs of discontent over a quiz that has sat in my car since Wednesday waiting to be graded have begun to be whispered. Little understanding exists for my plaintive pleas explaining that my cognitive state has not been up for grading the open-ended essay. Caroline is exhausted. Added to her plate is the need to pull together an Algebra I review from scratch. "Fake it until it's real" was my friend's motto. I'm running out of enough energy to even fake it.

(The Birthday Joys Continue)
5-21-2013
Tuesday

I just read in the paper today, that my measly 1% pay increase proposed by Governor Govern has been shot down by the Senate. This proves that the promise to ensure that our teachers and state employees are paid fairly, was merely a campaign promise and establishes why with unemployment hovering between the 9 -10% mark in Haversaw County, people aren't breaking down the doors to fill the two positions we still have open for next year in Haversaw's science department. According to the NEA, North Carolina ranks 49th in average teacher pay for the country. I'm just glad I don't work in Nebraska. For Pete's sake, even South Carolina and Mississippi pay teachers more than North Carolina!

Of course, when I later read the article about the tornadoes in Oklahoma, especially the story highlighted by the picture of the teacher kneeling in the ruble of his school, holding a traumatized child, I realized it could be a whole lot worse. At least I won't have to attend multiple funerals for my students. I cannot imagine what those poor souls are feeling at this moment.

To end on a pleasant note, Caroline's dad has had a good day. Some friends at school who are dealing with aging parents, one of whom has Alzheimer's, told me the bad times will come, so enjoy the times when they are feeling well.

5-22-2013
Wednesday

I'm stuck with a quandary. Yesterday my students scored so low on their test that I swear people in China could see their average. While I understand that it covered a large amount of material, their minds were on the prom, many students were involved in playoffs, and I was not at my best, it still makes me angry. I taught the material; they should be able to take a test, even if it covers a lot of material. My natural instincts are to leave the grades as is. I abhor extra credit and detest retests. I view both as rewards for the students screwing up. Sometimes learning means you have to realize that, no matter what is going on in your life, you still have obligations that need to be met. However, acids, bases, and solutions comprise almost an entire essential standard for the common exam. I can't afford to leave this material with the students' comprehension in this state of shambles. Some would argue that I should never leave a concept when over half the class fails a test, but I feel that the grade should reflect their work ethic and for this test, that ethic sucked. With less than a week of regular instruction left before exams start, I do not have the time to offer them a retest. So I'm stuck with test corrections. I still feel as if I'm rewarding them for not doing their part of the work.

We're finally at the end of the year. I have one more lesson to teach, and then it's review material from here on out. Caroline has finished up her Algebra I material as well. Her Calculus kids have been finished for over a week. The College Board, which administers the AP Exams, couldn't care less that North Carolina's tourist industry wanted us to start school August 25th—thereby continuing school well into June—because the Atlantic Ocean is warmer in August. Warmer water means more tourists, so who cares if late release and return is good for the students. The AP exams are given at the beginning of May, regardless of when a school system begins the year. So her kids have been watching Stand and Deliver, and enjoying it. Who knew kids could enjoy a movie that didn't have explosions?

With two days left in our regular schedule, Caroline and I are in a contest to see who will have the most interesting day tomorrow. She plans to spend the day duct taping her calculus books together as the kids return them. With the budget crunch, we haven't replaced math textbooks in nearly ten years. They're starting to show their age. The science textbooks are nearly seven years old, but mine look practically new. Seventeen years ago we had a biology textbook that was so pathetic I ditched it, preferring to build my own textbook. Now, I get to tailor-make it to match whatever goals and objectives happen to be in vogue at the time.

For my entry into the contest, I get to meet with a parent to discuss ways in which we (Note I said "we," not "he." That was the parent's quote on the phone today.) can improve his son's chemistry grade. Even though I pointed out that his son was missing a test from the end of April which he never made up, I only have two regular class days left, and I am only going to give two more quizzes, the father still wants to meet face to face to discuss matters. Given the fact that the man's last words to me were that his son is upset over not having the option of extra credit, leads me to speculate that the man intends to brow beat me into offering his son extra credit. I haven't done that in twenty years, and I don't intend to start tomorrow. Oh well, it should be a fun meeting.

5-23-2013
Thursday

Now, for the moment we've all been waiting for, the recap of yesterdays contest. Caroline used up quite a few rolls of duct tape. With books that old, she refuses to charge damage fees. I read in the paper today that the senate's budget has cut funds for new textbooks. I believe North Carolina is spending less than twenty dollars per student for textbooks. My chemistry textbook cost well over fifty dollars. The book allotment has been used solely for replacing books that were lost or were too damaged to be reissued. By now, the books can best be described as in pathetic condition. I wonder if the people making these decisions were required to use resources that were a decade old, would they provide the funds to replace the things in a timelier manner.

In the same paper was an article stating how the economy was improving. I can only speculate when it will finally trickle down to us? Oh wait, there was another article in the paper explaining how the NC senate is going to set aside several hundred million dollars to enact the tax reform for next year in which we have no idea how it will work, or if it will even be implemented. While I applaud the notion of fiscal responsibility, this is coming at the cost of replacing outdated books as well as eliminating yet more teaching positions. I'm wondering if I can get maintenance to hang hammocks up from my rafters to house the influx of yet more students into my room. So in order to put money aside for a program that may or may not become law, I will not have a pay increase (I wonder if we will be surpassed by Nebraska?), Caroline is holding her textbooks together with duct tape, and I may top 105 students in three classes. And people wonder why teachers are fed up.

I think Caroline won the contest. I was able to offer a compromise solution for the parent that I would have offered to any student. The father felt that he had accomplished something, and I didn't have to offer extra credit. It was a win-win situation. It's amazing what a little bit of compromising will do. Now will someone tell our elected leaders this little nugget of truth?

On a side note, I'm typing this in the bleachers of Kaitlyn's gym. While she is happily doing backbend kick-overs, I'm listening to two mothers jabber. Normally I would join into the discussion because we're all on friendly terms, but for this conversation I am reminded of a quote by Bugs Bunny. "If I dooed it, I'll get in trouble." Of course, Bugs proceeded to throw a pie in Elmer Fudd's face. For the sake of friendship, I chose not to "dooed it."

Their discussion wandered into the realm of schools, and it was not in a happy, magical tone in which they discussed their children's schools. No, this discourse was in the realms of "I can't believe how bad those teachers are." While offering a few caveats placing fault upon their own child, the vast majority of blame was laid at the feet of the teachers. They proceeded to offer ways in which the school should be run, pointed out the fallacies of the teachers who have tried to educate their children, and offered anecdotal stories of people blessing out the teachers, some of which bordered into the areas of abuse.

I have a fantasy that when I retire, I am going to pick up the phone, call random companies, and tell whoever has the misfortune to answer how they are pathetic excuses of human beings who should be fired because they are so incompetent they cannot solve problems over which they have no control. Of course, I would never actually do this, but it does make me mad when people who have never set foot in a school feel they are experts on childhood education simply because they have raised kids. Never once is consideration given to the fact that there is a tremendous difference in raising one to four kids and teaching 20 to 30 kids. When it's your own kids, you can control the rewards and punishments. When it's someone else's kids, you get, "How dare you treat my child as if he/she did anything wrong." A lot of the complaints I heard could be contributed to overcrowded classes, an administration whose hands are tied for fear of repercussions of any disciplinary actions, an unyielding computer scheduling program, and the mandated tests.

One mother could not understand why the principal would move the good teacher from her daughter's classroom to a third-grade classroom where a teacher had suddenly quit. The long-term substitute teacher was placed in the daughter's second grade class. The answer is simple, and it's one that most parents and elected officials have created. The standardized tests that are used to evaluate the performance of the students, the teachers, and the schools don't factor in the case of a teacher quitting. There is no place to enter in data such as "teacher left and substitute took over." If the scores drop, there's hell to pay. So, good teachers are moved into classes that have high-stakes tests so the principal doesn't lose his or her job. We also don't get a break if a child moves into our class with two weeks left in the school year. Their name is on your roster, their scores are calculated in your evaluation and the overall school performance.

So for the sake of friendship, I'm going to keep my mouth shut. Like Bugs said, "If I dooed it, I'll get in trouble."

People ask me why I am against performance-based pay using test scores as a measure of my effectiveness. I've already documented the state of North Carolina's reluctance to pay me my bonus money (i.e. merit-based pay) based on the school's overall performance on the state mandated standardized test scores, so I'll try to refrain from whining anymore about that topic. However, today exemplifies another reason why I am against this practice. It was Awards Day at Haversaw High. Whether it is referred to as Awards Day, Class Day, Senior Recognition Day, etc., this is the day where the seniors assemble as a class in honor of all of their achievements. For the administration this is a day for the underclassmen to be inspired by the accomplishments of the senior class, so they, like the students before them, will aspire to greatness.

The underclassmen, however, view it slightly differently. For them, it is a day of torture where they are forced to watch people they don't know walk up to get some award the underclassmen couldn't care less about. To further compound the problem, the only area big enough to house the entire student population plus parents of the seniors is the gym, which lacks air-conditioning. Today marks our highest rate of absences during the entire year.

This year Mr. Flair bowed down to the demands of the teachers and allowed us to keep our kids in class during Awards Day if they were not seniors. I might add that my students met this announcement with a round of applause. As I said, the students view this event slightly differently than the administration.

I had scheduled a review quiz plus handing out the final exam review packet. Even though the kids knew we were having a quiz, I still had a high rate of absenteeism. Apparently the lure of a four-day weekend held more sway in the minds of my students than reviewing for an exam upon which my effectiveness is judged. Of the kids who were physically present, their minds were on distant shores basking in the warm summer sun. It was a long day, with many a growl to keep the kids focused upon net ionic equations and stoichiometry.

Therein lies the problem with basing the effectiveness of a teacher on one test. These are kids, not machines. In a company, if the product doesn't work, you toss it out. I can't do that with my kids. I'm trying everything I can to keep these kids focused, but I can't compete with four-day weekends and dreams of summer. And let's face it, some of the absent kids were home screwing their brains out. As I said, I can't compete.

In the workplace the employer holds a paycheck over a worker's head. While in theory, that is what's happening with me, there is an important difference. I'm not pushing paper, making devices, etc. I have to work with humans and I don't have anything to hold over their heads. Yes, I could remind them that their exam grade is 25% of their average, but when a student has a 30 average and the alternative to staying at school studying for an exam is staying home to have sex with his girlfriend, then I'm doomed. So next time you are so quick to pass judgment upon a teacher because of poor test scores, allow me to base your next performance review on the actions of ninety hormone-driven teenagers who would rather be anywhere else in the known universe than taking the test upon which you are judged.

5-27-2013
Memorial Day

It's amazing what three days of rest, the kids' activities winding down, and plenty of sleep will do for you. But while Memorial Day has become known as a day of picnics, grilling, and the unofficial kick-off to summer, we must not forget the real importance of this day. We must not forget those who gave their lives for our country.

10

The First Day of Exams, I think.

5-28-2013
Tuesday

You know it's bad when you are up until past midnight tossing and turning worrying if you are giving an exam in the morning. Before you leap to the conclusion that I am either a blubbering idiot (the conclusion favored by my students) or have lost my mind (the conclusion favored by my friends), let me explain my confusion. We have three separate schedules for high schools in the Haversaw School System. At Haversaw High and other "normal" high schools, we have been cursed with a hybrid schedule of semester block classes that meet for ninety-minutes every day of the week and yearlong A-day, B-day classes that meet for ninety-minutes every other day. All of my classes are semester classes while all of Caroline's classes are A-day/B-day classes. So, you can't simply say Tuesday will be the day for first period exams. Which first period are you referring to: Semester first periods, A-day first periods, or B-day first period? To further muddy the waters, we are offering three different types of exams. For the testing pleasures of our students, we offer teacher-made exams, End-Of-Course exams, and Common Exams. There is actually a fourth type of exam for the business teachers called CTEs, but they are lumped in with the EOCs and, thankfully, do not need a separate schedule. Each test has a different set of requirements and are, in essence, given on a separate day although some overlap does exist.

The Common Exams, which I'm giving, have a minimum time allotment of ninety minutes, which will fit nicely into a regular block class. In order to accommodate the reading of directions,

CE exam blocs are two hours long. These are being given this week. So we're on a bizarre schedule cobbled together with the same results as Frankenstein's monster. Today, Haversaw students will take their 1-A, and 3-A common exams. Normally, this would mean my first and third period students would take an exam. Instead, we're having class. Tomorrow, during the 1-B and 3-B exam slots, is when my kiddies are taking their exams. Today is my last review day with my third period class. I have first period planning, so at least I had time to figure out all of this madness, although there is a chance that I could be called upon to either proctor an exam or give an exam for a CE teacher who is absent. I could only sit in on CEs because I have not been trained in the proper methods for administering the other types of tests. If I even set foot in an EOC exam, I would cause a misadministration due to the fact that I had not been trained to be in the same room with the tests. Confused yet?

Thursday and Friday, we will offer our second and fourth period exams. Now, in years past, once the kids took their exams, they were done with the course. However, this year, I get to see my classes six more times after they have completed the course. The frustrating thing is our administration is telling us to offer graded assignments for the kids. I'm okay with this and have planned to run a few of the longer duration labs I was not able to do during the semester. However, the frustration enters into the picture when they also have me scheduled to be pulled out of my classes to grade the essays of Common Exams. As far as I can tell, I'm supposed to continue to have class. The administration is secretly hoping that the kids will stay home, even though we can't tell them to stay home because we're pretty certain that violates some law or decree.

Next we enter into phase II of the exam schedule. This is the time of the EOCs and CTEs. These tests have a four-hour time limit, so it is physically impossible to offer two of them in a day. So we will have EOCs/CTEs in the morning. Now, if you do not have an EOC, then you will give your teacher made exam during that morning block of time unless you have A-day/B-day classes, which will have one class's exam in the four-hour block in the morning, and the other day's class will have a two-hour exam in the afternoon. As a result, Caroline has to prepare an exam that will take both two and four hours of time for her students to complete. Me, I'm going to teach a regular class while I'm also in the library grading CEs. I'm assuming Mr. Flair has a cloning machine stashed away in the supply closet.

To further complicate matters, we have a random A-day worked into the schedule on June 4th for reasons unknown to anybody and exam make-up days/regular class days on June 10th and 11th, which are snow make-up days. Nobody knows what the hell we're supposed to do on those days.

To top this lovely cake of confusion and uncertainty, we have a career and technical high school in the system that offers courses students cannot take at their "home" school. Students drive from all of the other schools across the county to take any number of classes at this institution. I have students in my chemistry classes who are at the technical school during the morning and then drive to Haversaw for their afternoon classes. This school is on an eight-period schedule, which throws the proverbial monkey wrench into everything because this school is on an entirely different exam schedule.

I hope this clarifies why I laid awake last night worrying if I was giving an exam today.

5-30-2013
Thursday

Initial indications on the CE are matching what I expected. The kids I anticipated would do well, felt like the test was easy, with the exception of Amanda who thinks every test is hard and still manages to make no grade below a 99 on them. The kids I expected to have trouble with the test thought it was difficult. A few kids were upset over some of the questions.

Now here's a frustrating thing about these exams. Outside of general feelings of difficulty by my students, I can't discuss the test questions with the kids. It is considered unethical to actually help the kids understand a concept that troubles them. However, it is perfectly ethical to hold the students and teachers accountable for a test that I have never seen and can only guess from vaguely worded goals and standards as to its content.

All in all, I was pleased. My best students felt that there were only four questions for which they were clueless. This really isn't bad considering someone else wrote the questions, and I will never see the multiple-choice portion of the test. Hopefully, this will bode well for the students and me. Maybe, just maybe, I'll get one of those non-funded, merit-based pay raises our general assembly and governor keep mentioning.

5-31-2013
Friday

Four days of giving Common Exams, and I have managed to make it without triggering a misadministration. Given the choice between dealing with a teacher killing a child or a teacher causing a misadministration, I cannot predict, with confidence, which a principal would choose. When a misadministration occurs, the entire class' tests are destroyed and everyone must return for another test session. Misadministrations usually appear in the paper with less than complimentary commentary. To say it is a hassle is comparable to saying the Titanic sprung a little leak. It's a nightmare. So, after I turned my last set of exams into the maelstrom that is test central at Haversaw High, I breathed a huge sigh of relief.

Non-teaching friends have asked what it is like to give an exam, falsely claiming they would love to get paid to sit on their butts doing nothing. I assure them that they would not enjoy it. Solitary confinement is a nasty punishment for a reason. While test administration is not, by definition, solitary, you are prohibited from interacting with all of humanity for the duration of the tests. Even your interactions with the students are scripted. It was felt that some teachers gave their students an unfair advantage by paraphrasing the exam directions, so we are now required to recite the litany of directions prepared by the state. By the third day, you are saying them in your sleep. A friend of mine is heading to a review board at the end of the school year for speeding through the directions for a kid who arrived late for a make-up exam. In an attempt to give the child enough time on his test, she skipped the parts of the directions pertaining to bubbling in circles on the answer sheet. The child is EC and has a modification where he marks his answers in his test books, and a scribe fills in the bubbles later under the watchful eye of two other administrations. For this omission, the board must decide if she will be reprimanded for paraphrasing the directions, or if she will be suspended without pay. Even though remote, the possibility of firing is not out of the realms of possibility. When teachers say the testing is stressful, they aren't kidding.

Once I successfully read the directions, I experienced the sheer joy of watching kids take a test. Trapped in a room with absolutely nothing to do but stare at students frantically trying to answer questions concerning topics ranging from electrons to gerunds. Forbidden to read, write, or do yoga, my existence fell into a pattern. Ten minutes elapsed, time to walk around the room. Another ten minutes, circle the room in the opposite direction. Another ten minutes elapsed, glance to see on what number the kids are currently working. After another ten minutes, repeat the process.

During the third or fourth cycle, my mind began to wander. My consciousness kept getting drawn to the inspirational poster adorning Mr. X's wall. Fearful that teachers may give nonverbal clues to their students, Haversaw School System mandated that teachers would no longer give a state test to their own students unless a trained proctor was in the room. Due to the sheer volume of Common Exams, our testing coordinator could not arrange enough proctors for all of them. So I'm giving an exam to kids I don't know to prohibit Mr. X from coughing in a specific manner to give away an answer for a test he hasn't read. Our society has sunk to this level.

But, I digress from the narrative. During the third or fourth cycle, my mind began to wander, and I found myself strangely drawn toward the inspirational poster of a schooner sitting idle in becalmed seas. The window in the classroom door became the porthole of my ship, providing my only view to the world at large. Faint blurs of movement proved that the world still existed beyond the scope of my limited purview. All too quickly, the blurs moved on into the sea of my imagination, never to be identified, and thus adding to my torment.

Anyway, you get the picture. Administering a state test is extremely boring. Most teachers resort to mind tricks to prevent them from falling into the mental trap I just described. They count shoes, compare various shades of toenail polish, analyze fashion trends demonstrated in the classroom, and so on. I've been known to design entire kingdoms in my head, complete with epic battles dominating their history. We do what we need to do to pass the time and keep our sanity.

All of this has been brought about by various problems that have occurred in the past. While I've never been guilty of the causing a disturbance during an exam, I can more than understand how difficult it must be to take a test worth 25% of your grade while your teacher is loudly discussing with a friend the volatility of North Carolina politics. Still, it makes for an extremely boring day. Incidentally, in case you were wondering, in this particular class, 20% of the students wore sandals, 55% wore sneakers, 10% wore loafers, 5% wore some type of flat dress shoe, and 10% were sporting flip-flops.

6-7-2013
The Last Day of Testing.
We Think.

Sorry for the delay in writing, but I received a wonderful gift from my students in the form of a cold and sinus infection. "Yuck" is the best description of how I've felt for the past week. Let's just say that ending the year with a sinus infection is not fun. To further compound the problem, Caroline's dad was just admitted to the hospital with pneumonia—in both lungs—which his doctors speculate he may have acquired during his previous stay. I've come home and collapsed for the past three days.

My exams were over last week, but I still had classes due a quirk in the Haversaw schedule and the fact that we have three different types of exams, which I explained earlier. This week, much to the chagrin of my students, I had the audacity to continue with my lessons. It gave me a chance to complete of couple of labs that I just couldn't work into the schedule, although, if the truth were known, I would have rather had the time before they took their exam. But, that's the joy of mandated testing—you don't always get what you want.

Graduation is tomorrow, and thankfully all of my seniors passed chemistry. North Carolina has a nasty little twist in graduation requirements. If you skip Physical Science, you must pass Physics or Chemistry or you don't graduate. For some of my seniors, they cut it close. I hate it when I'm the reason a kid doesn't walk across the stage.

6-08-2013
Graduation

As has happened numerous times this year, when I had envisioned writing about a certain topic, the reality was far different from my earlier vision. Graduation was yet one more example of this concept. At the start of this project, I had planned to discuss the feelings of pride teachers feel as the kids line up to walk into the stadium, knowing they had played a part in turning these savage children into adults. High school teachers yearn for this moment, the moment when they know their endeavors have made a difference in the lives of their students. This feeling is so deeply rooted in teachers that many will clamor for a graduation duty where they are out in the crowds, celebrating with the parents.

Personally, I prefer to work behind the scenes. Frivolity and joviality are the norm, as these students prepare for the start of their adult lives. They are excited, sad, eager, and scared, all at once. This is what I like to recall of graduations. It gives me one last chance to be Mr. Gregory with my students. Once they cross the stage, I have told them to address me as William. They've earned the right.

However, this year I was an emotional and physical wreck. I calculated that I had slept 10 hours in a 72-hour span of time. My sinus infection had descended into my upper chest, and bouts of coughing were punctuated with hoarse whispers of frustrations. It was all I could muster. Underlying everything, was the fear we all felt for Caroline's father. After 24-hours of two different IV antibiotics, his condition has deteriorated. While he is alert and will carry on a conversation as well as anyone can who is nearly deaf and blind, he has not responded to the treatments. The nurses have refused to comment, but the look in their eyes belies their assurances that all is well. When Caroline checked, Buck was now on four liters per minute of oxygen. He was receiving half that amount when he entered the hospital. For me, at least, graduation was not the festive occasion it usually is.

My job, this graduation, was to guard an exit of the stadium leading into a storage area for the grounds equipment. It was up to me to prevent the parents from wandering into this area and possibly getting hurt. Needless to say, this task did not need my immediate attention, so I meandered into the staging area for the students. It was here that my worries faded into the background and I was able to joke around with my soon-to-be former students. Between cries of "Mr. Gregory" and responses of "You did it!" I was once again Mr. Gregory the teacher, with nary a care other than enjoying this last minute with my Haversaw kids.

All too soon, I returned to my post and became just another spectator in a suit, indistinguishable from all of the other proud parents. Blending in allowed me to observe the rest of humanity rushing to get a seat and helping grandparents navigate the crowds. I was a part, yet isolated from them as well. As the ceremony began, and amid catcalls from exuberant family members, I wondered about my future. It had been a hard year for teachers on the political front in North Carolina. Numerous friends were leaving the profession, and we haven't been able to fill their positions. Masters pay for new teachers has been cut, and the proposed raise by our governor was removed from the budget. Class sizes have increased, and may get larger yet.

It is a scary time for education. Despair along this line of thought led my thoughts back to Buck. Caroline's last update had the amount of oxygen supplied to him rising again. While concerns for my future were important, my thoughts were brought back into focus. I'm left with the irony that I'm witnessing a beginning for my students while I'm afraid I may be seeing an ending for my father in-law. The last word we received from the doctors was that Buck would probably have to go to a skilled nursing home when he is released from the hospital. As I said earlier, this was not the ending of the school year I had envisioned in August.

6-11-2013
The last day of school.

Yes, it's after graduation, but with snow make-ups, we do what we must.

It's the last day of school. The only kids present are those who couldn't con their mothers into letting them stay home. The state of North Carolina says we have to have 180 days and 1000 hours of quality instructional time, so here we are. So far I have had four kids in my second period class, three kids in my third period, and one lost soul in my fourth period.

Sandy's room is packed up. It's amazing how much "stuff" we accumulate in teaching. If anyone thinks the $200 tax credit given to teachers for the purchase of classroom supplies is too generous, they should visit a classroom. While it is frowned upon by the principal and police for teachers to accidentally acquire supplies bought by the school, items purchased by Sandy have been stored in boxes, ready to be transported to her new school. She's excited about her new job. I'm not. I hate goodbyes.

Buck's pneumonia turned out to be something far worse. You do not want to hear the word's "interstitial lung disease" come from the mouth of your doctor. By lunch, Buck had deteriorated to the point where the doctors wanted to put him on a ventilator. Caroline rushed to the hospital when her brother sent word. There are times when school's importance pales in comparison to what is occurring in a teacher's life. If anyone wishes to be critical of her decision, Caroline's other brother, a prominent businessman, left a high-stakes business trip overseas to travel home.

To add insult to injury, after recovering from my sinus infection, I've picked up a cold virus from the hospital.

So, on the last day of school, I'm snotty, my best friend at Haversaw is leaving, and Caroline just called to tell me that hospice has been called. This just sucks.

6-12-2013
Wednesday

For the past few days, I've lived in a bizarre state, existing in two worlds. The first consisted of the teacher trying to finish out the school year. All of those mundane tasks necessary to shut your room down for the summer needed to be done. Equipment had to be stored, books counted and shelved, grades posted, desks numbered so the cleaning crew wouldn't lose them over the summer, etc. All of this has to be completed, and I worked as a zombie on each task. Sleep has not been high on my priority list in the past 24 hours.

All the while, my thoughts were focused on the drama unfolding ten short miles away. I was at work today, thinking fate would allow me a few hours to check some things off of my list when Caroline called shortly after 1:00 p.m. Sobbing, she choked out the simple words, "He's dead." Throwing the last odds and ends into cabinets, I rushed out as soon as I received assurances from Jennifer that she would take care of Mckenzie and Kaitlyn who were at the school helping me.

This sums up the life of a teacher. We live in two worlds. In one, we are the face of the state. We're entrusted with the care and education of society's children, we enforce authority, and dispatch compassion. We're revered and reviled, and we do all of this out of a dedication to our calling.

We are also people. We have families of our own. Life's ups and downs intrude into our lives. We pay taxes, have mortgages, provide taxi services for our kids, and suffer through countless hours of homework trying to figure out why our daughter picked "The History of Forks" for her presentation topic. We celebrate when life enters the world and grieve when it departs.

We are not the villains portrayed by some aspects of the media. We are not money-hungry parasites trying to deprive the state of its precious tax dollars, striving to receive pay increase after pay increase for doing nothing while gleefully watching kids fail in their academic endeavors.

Nor are we superheroes, raised to standards few humans could dare to reach. We touch lives, yet we see a child for a precious little amount of time. Realistically, the miracles portrayed in *Dead Poets Society* and *Stand and Deliver* are few and far between. This is not from lack of effort on the part of the teacher, but from the reality that life encroaches upon the student as much as it does the teacher. When a student is hungry and slept on the couch of a friend because her mom's boyfriend pimped her mother out to pay for his crack addiction, that student couldn't care less about which subatomic particle orbits the nucleus of an atom. I've seen horrors like this many times and will see more before I retire. Schools fail because society has failed these kids. Given that fact, the teachers who work in failing schools strive endlessly to stave off this failure, knowing that for all of their efforts, they will receive nothing but blame.

Years ago, my roommate in college served as a volunteer firefighter. His favorite quote was, "You know most people run away from a burning building. We're the crazy #$%^* who run into the burning building." That is an apt description for teachers as well. According to the more hate-filled rhetoric, the very fabric of American society is crumbling. Well, we're the crazy #$%^* who rush into the societal collapse thinking we can make a difference in the life of a kid. I'm a teacher and I'm damn proud of what I do.

11

Reflections

Ask anyone who has ever led an educational conference, workshop, or staff development, and he or she will say that reflecting upon past and new practices is essential to growth as a teacher. I can't say that I agree with the statement, and I usually create Grade-A fertilizer when I write a reflection, but this work seemed to call for a discussion upon prominent themes that arose during the course of the 2012-2013 school year.

First, teachers are human with the same foibles and prone to the same fallacies that are associated with the rest of our race. Simply by entering the classroom does not erase that humanity. We fight amongst ourselves, and the same drama and backstabbing we all experienced and loved in junior high is still alive almost thirty years later. However, every teacher I know strives to do what is best for his or her students. We're humans with a passion for teaching, not monsters preying upon the innocent victims, i.e., our students.

At some point in my twenty years of teaching, I've gone from being a public servant to being public enemy number one in the minds of our elected officials. I don't know why. An indication of this came last year when the General Assembly passed a bill making it illegal for the NCAE (the state level branch of the NEA: National Educators Association) to collect member dues through paycheck withdrawal, a practice that had been in effect for my entire career and is still in effect for most other professional organizations in other branches of government jobs. During the lead-up to the vote, the Speaker was overheard through an open microphone as saying "The reason we've decided to do that is the NCAE has gone into all five districts with mailers hammering those Democrats [those Democrats being the ones who sided with the Speaker on a previous issue]... we just want to give them a little taste about what's to come." (http://www.maconnews.com/opinion/2418-reactionary-legislature-punishes-teachers) Since then, teachers have suffered through stagnant pay, the elimination of increased pay for a master's degree for new teachers, increased work loads, increased class sizes, the humiliation of the possible removal of the protection of due process for job protection, and being linked as parasites on the public coffers by various media personalities. To me, this seems to exemplify the adage, "With friends like these, who needs enemies?"

The second theme that emerged consists of education reform. While education reform is great, it doesn't replace the tried-and-true methods that, despite the media's claim to the contrary, worked. It was these same methods that produced the people who led our nation through the turmoil of two World Wars, The Great Depression, and the Cold War. These methods of teaching also inspired the scientists who created our technological-oriented world and sent humans to the moon. While, yes the world has changed, I do not think we, as a state and nation, need to bounce from one education reform technique to another simply for the sake of doing something different. We need to conscientiously evaluate all teaching methods to analyze what works. All teachers have their own styles of teaching. It is an injustice to force us into some collective style of education pedagogy simply for the sake of uniformity. When analyzed objectively, we must consider the very real possibility that it is both mutually exclusive goals and flawed methods of collecting data that have created the education crisis touted in the media.

Above all else, you cannot test your way into true reform. Politicians, the media, and even parents have now started to confuse standardized tests with reform. True teaching cannot be quantified, and critical thinking cannot be evaluated with a multiple-choice test. On top of this fallacy in collecting the data to damn teachers and schools, we've reached a point where it is entirely plausible to say that our students suffer through almost a month of standardized testing within the course of a school year. This is both ridiculous and counterproductive to true education reform where our students are taught how to be productive, rational, and cognizant adults.

My third point, and a sad attempt to capitalize on a crude pun, is that size does matter. I don't care how it looks on the record books, but just one more kid in a classroom makes a huge difference when your numbers are above 25. In my earth science classes, the majority of my class time was spent with crowd control. There were simply too many bodies for me to effectively separate the troublemakers. True education reform begins with reducing class sizes. Unless politicians are willing to supply the funds to bring our class sizes down to fewer than 25 students, then their calls for reform are meaningless.

The fourth theme that I have discovered through this process is one that nobody wants to admit exists. The type of kid makes a difference. When you have to fight kids the entire day, and your class time is spent with discipline issues, you're going to have lousy days. This may explain why teachers flee poor performing schools. There is only so much you can take. When you take troubled kids from troubled schools and put them in good schools, they don't miraculously become model students. Often, they bring the trouble with them. A friend of mine witnessed this in his classroom when he had to breakup a bullying ring involving multiple kids, all of whom were attending Haversaw High even though they lived out of district and came from troubled schools.

If parents and legislatures truly want to address school reform, simply allowing students to switch schools is not the solution. It only hides the problem. True reform must occur at home. The parents of unruly kids have to accept responsibility and rein in their kids. I cannot begin to count the number of times I have talked to parents concerning their child's behavior only to have the response of "I can't do anything with him at home." Well, if the parents can't do anything with their children, what do they expect teachers to be able to do? We're not miracle workers, especially when the politicians tie our hands over discipline issues. Once teachers can stop being the parents of other people's children, then we can begin to teach again.

Finally, teachers can take a lot of abuse, but when you start cutting the benefits we were promised, the abuse looks less inviting. Time and time again, my journal reflected the fear of losing my pension and the frustration of stagnant pay. For the first time in our careers, Caroline has begun to discuss the possibility of retiring early and seeking employment elsewhere. In her mind, we might as well start drawing retirement before the option is removed.

Teachers are people. We have families to support. The stagnant pay is now necessitating the need to reevaluate the activities in which the Gregory girls will be able to participate. While our pay has been in stasis, the cost of dance, gymnastics, orange juice, etc. has not. Are teachers frustrated? Hell, yes. Just because we chose to enter public service should not force us to choose between buying food and enriching our children's lives. Whether we are ranked 49th in teacher pay, or 46th as a recent news story reported, it is still pathetic for North Carolina to pay its teachers so poorly. Elected officials pay lip service to the idea that children come first, but their actions in paying the people whose jobs is to ensure this state otherwise.

I recently read an article predicting that the salary freeze would result in teachers leaving NC for other states. While I was at the AP Environmental Science workshop, attended by a high number of young teachers, I observed the fruition of this prediction. Many of the younger teachers were in NC for the sole purpose of gaining experience, and they planned to leave as soon as they could find a job in another state. I advised any who would listen that, as far as I could see, they were crazy to continue to work in this state when they could earn anywhere from $5,000 to $10,000 more a year in other states.

This sums up the frustrations that have built up over the years. Twenty years ago, I would never have thought of leaving North Carolina. While not the state of my birth, it became my home. Between elected officials who seem to view teachers as targets to be eliminated, to unattainable educational goals due to the fact that to achieve one, the other must fail, to the elimination of tenure, to the possible elimination of my pension fund, to over-crowding in poorly funded classrooms, to stagnant pay, it is only the fact of my twenty years of service and the need to provide care for aging parents that hold Caroline and me here. I hope things will change, I hope sanity will be restored, and I desper-ately hope I get a pay increase before I retire, but I cannot see it on the foreseeable horizon. Am I fed up with the situation? Hell, yes. We, as a society, have taken my job of teaching, which I love, and broken it, possibly beyond repair.

I'm a fed-up teacher, angry, and possibly a little desperate. Yet, that glimmer of excitement is already starting to build for the next school year, the anticipation of meeting a new set of kids, and the undying hope of making a difference in the lives of the kids of North Carolina. As I said, I'm a teacher, and I'm damn proud of it.

Chip Putnam

A 1993 graduate of UNC Charlotte, Chip has dedicated the past 22 years to teaching high school science. He has had the pleasure of meeting wonderful and fascinating people in that time who have provided inspiration for many characters in his writing. While the field of science is not the area of expertise normally associated with an aspiring author, he has always been a dreamer and would often enter into the world of his own imagination at a moment's notice. This love of dreaming—coupled with a passion for books plus a tendency to weave storytelling into his lessons—created in him a desire to write. Building on the encouragement he had given to countless students, he followed his own dream, and his first book, *Diary of a Fed Up Teacher*, was published in 2014 (SWP) and republished in 2016 by Prospective Press. *The Guardians of Knowledge* is his second book, published in 2015 by Prospective Press.

He received honorable mention from the 2011 Words of Love contest sponsored by the Writer's Workshop of Asheville, NC for the short story A Lesson in Love at Haversaw High. In 2012, his short story, *The Cat's in the Cradle Curio Shop* won first place in a Fanstory.com postcard story contest, and was published on the website Postcard Shorts. In 2012, his short story, *The Reason Why Grandmothers Should Not Be Allowed To Read Vampire Novels* placed second in a Fanstory.com panel reviewed contest. Also in 2012, he was a finalist out of 1,400 entries in a Writer's Digest "First Things First" contest for writing a prompted opening sentence. The finalists' opening sentences are printed in the January 2013 edition of Writer's Digest. Two of his short stories, *Why Grandmas Shouldn't Be Allowed To Read Vampire Stories* and *Prairie Zombies*, are included in the anthology *Off The Beaten Path 1* published by Prospective Press. Most recently, his manuscript "Mr. Judy: The Advice Man" advanced to the Quarter Finalist stage of the 2014 Amazon Breakthrough Novel Awards.

He has been married for twenty years and has two children. He lives in North Carolina.